Work in Progress

BJ HARVEY
USA Today Bestselling Author

Chapter One

Jamie

I TAKE ANOTHER SWIG FROM my beer, then drop it down onto the wood floor. After picking up the hammer, I hook an exposed nail and yank it out of its home.

Demo isn't due to begin until tomorrow, but with nothing else to do with my night, I decided to come over, sleep on the floor, and get a head start.

Moving sideways a foot, I repeat the action—minus the beer this time. It's rinse and repeat until I finish removing the rotting trim lining the small wall, letting Queen blast through my head as I grab my drink, finish the bottle, and put it to the side.

This is what I've needed: time by myself, loud music, a few beers, and "dick stuff," as my sister, Abi, eloquently calls it.

It just so happens that there's a lot of "dick stuff" to be done now that I've sunk most of my savings into the worst house on a fairly good suburban street.

When Heather, my girlfriend of three years, dumped me out of the blue, spewed unexpected vitriol my way and blamed me for how our lives had turned out, I re-evaluated. Not her—as far as I'm concerned, it's a blessing I saw her true colors in that break-up speech before it was too late. The engagement ring was bought, and plans for a wedding proposal were in progress, but finding out the woman you love thinks you're a loser with no ambition and she can't wait to be rid of you makes a man take note.

That brings me to the house I'm standing in the middle of. I've always loved working with my hands, and having spent the last ten years of my life as a boat captain—and newly single—I decided to bite the bullet. So I quit my job, worked for my friend's construction company for a few months, and decided to put my money where my dreams were, flipping houses. With a three-month turnaround, the aim is to eventually make a real go of this. Starting with this three-bed, one-bath bungalow.

It's not just me doing this though, which is a blessing and a curse. My three younger brothers decided to pitch their tent next to mine—figuratively—and while they all still have their own jobs as backup, they have each shown they have faith in me to succeed by investing in the company and pledging to help me whenever they can. So I now have the pressure of not screwing my family's future up while not completely destroying my own. Oh, and the small matter of having absolutely no fallback if this fails.

No pressure or anything.

My back pocket vibrates, and I pull out my phone, seeing my friend Jase's name on the screen as I walk into the kitchen and away from the music.

Jase recently married the love of his life and an amazing woman, Natalie, in a surprise wedding he planned using her own dream wedding book. It was no easy feat considering he made her think they were having a Chicago Bears ceremony at Soldier Field.

Thankfully for everyone involved, it was a very well-thought-out ruse to hide what he truly wanted, and in the end—although there was no doubt in anyone's minds—he got the girl, the wife, and a wedding night in a giant tent on her parents' Indiana farm.

"Hey, you came up for air?" I say with a smile. He chuckles, and I can imagine the big shit-eating grin on his face right now.

"I'm barely clinging onto life," Jase replies. "I love my wife more than anything in this world, but that woman is like a nymphomaniac overdosing on female Viagra. My dick feels like it's gonna go on strike just to give itself time to recover."

"There are worse ways to go, my friend."

"Ain't that the truth? One day, you'll meet a woman who'll knock you on your ass," he says with a laugh. "So how's Maple going?" Maple being the street on which this undiscovered gem of a house I'm currently renovating lies. Jase and our other friend Matt own a construction company, and we'll all be working together on this project. Again, no pressure.

"I've discovered a few things I'll need you and Matt to come take a look at, but otherwise, it seems a bit overwhelming as a whole. There's just a lot to do."

"It always seems like that, but once we have a clear plan in place, it won't seem so mammoth."

"I'll take your word for that," I say, notching the phone between my head and my shoulder and moving along to start the next panel.

"Promise you, Jamie. It'll run like clockwork once we get started."

"I hope you're right," I grunt, hooking the hammer under the lip of the trim and jerking it back. When it only moves an inch, I wedge the fingers of my other hand between the wood and the drywall. As I give it an almighty tug, a loud knock at the door throws me off and the hammer slips, slicing my palm open a good inch and a half.

"Fuck!" My loud bellow echoes around the empty room while burning pain cuts through me.

"Jamie? What the fu—" The phone crashes to the ground as I grab my hand and squeeze tight.

As I slide my back down the wall, I look around for something—anything—to soak up the gushing blood.

Then the front door swings open, and a woman I've never seen before—but wish I had—fills the void.

"Oh hell," she says, running across the room to kneel down beside me. "Do you have a first-aid kit?" Her eyes taking in the scene in front of her.

"You might find one of my T-shirts in the other room, but that's about it," I reply. She nods, stopping by the speaker and turning it all the way down before disappearing down the short hallway.

She returns a few moments later, my green tee clutched in her hand. Her brows are pinched together as she assesses the scene in front of her. I have to admit, it probably looks bad. Loud music, beer bottles, a random man with no clue doing demolition late on a Thursday night.

"Who are you?" I ask, remembering this woman is a total stranger who effectively barged through my door. I'm grateful, but a little confused. She stuffs my T-shirt onto the wound and presses down firmly.

"We haven't met. I'm Jamie." I offer my uninjured hand her way.

"And I'm the neighbor who was coming over to yell at you to stop making so much noise," she says with a sigh. "Which is just as well, considering *that*. You're lucky you've got a nurse living next door." She nods at my hand before squaring me with a look that would probably make a less-drunk man shake in his sneakers. But I've always felt untouchable with too many drinks under my belt.

She has the most amazing piercing blue eyes I've ever seen. There's a fiery spark to them that any man would want to set alight. It's probably her anger causing it, but it makes me think of all the other things that could make her glow.

Even the scowl she's shooting my way is hot. I bet her husband has to fight going hard whenever they have a fight.

All thoughts of my damaged hand vanish in that moment as I take in her outfit. I scan her from the dark brown hair tied in a messy mop on top of her head, to her oversized blue tee paired with pajama pants covered in… sloths? I have to bite back a laugh.

"What are you smiling at?" she asks tersely.

"Sloths?" I ask, my eyes dropping to her curvy hips. Damn, if she has a tattoo anywhere on that body, I'll be a goner.

Her eyes narrow on mine. "You're worried about what I'm wearing when you've got a gash here that probably needs stitches."

I shrug, unable to look away. I try to catch a glance of her ring finger. That would be just my fucking luck. A gorgeous—albeit aggravated—woman literally pushes her way into my life, and she's probably taken. "My brother is an EMT; he can fix me right up."

"Or maybe you can think twice before doing demolition while drunk next time," she snaps. "But then again, evidence suggests you're not a man who thinks things through."

My shoulders turn to stone. "What makes you say that?" I ask—the audacity of this damn woman. I try to pull my arm away, but she reads me like a book and tightens her grip.

She levels me with a glare. "Stubborn too, I see?"

My mouth drops open. Why haven't I kicked her out of my house already?

I hold her gaze, initiating a silent standoff that I'm compelled to win. She gives as good as she gets and doesn't back down. I bet if we were standing, her hands would be firmly on her hips and I'd be fighting not to go hard at the promise of igniting that sass in other more creative and enjoyable ways.

I shake my head because the last thing I want or need right now is a distraction to derail my plans. I look away but not before I catch a sly smile playing on her lips as she returns her attention to my injured hand. She pulls back the fabric to assess the damage, and I hide my wince as the cool air stings the wound. I study her face as she puts pressure on my skin again.

"Are you married?" I ask.

Her gaze snaps back to mine, her fingers jerking against my palm. "What?"

"Married? Husband? Are you with someone?" I ramble.

Her lips twitch, and she quirks a brow. "What if I have a wife?"

Shit. I didn't think of that.

"Well… ah… um…" I stutter.

She winks at me at the same time as she tightens her grip over the cut.

"Fuck," I groan. My wide eyes jump to hers. "Shit. Sorry. My mother would have my ass if she heard me cursing in front of a stranger."

The woman moves her head closer to mine, those dazzling eyes of hers now dancing. "I won't tell her if you don't," she whispers before leaning back. "I happen to love cussing… at the right time, of course."

Wait, is she flirting with me? I've been out of the game for years; have the rules changed? Was there a dating memo I missed? She never did answer the married question, did she? And why did this all happen to me after a few too many beers?

If I were a bit more clear-headed, I definitely wouldn't be unsure of myself, but alcohol lowers my defenses. It always has. It's not that it gets me in trouble, but I'm the first to admit that it has an effect on my usual cocky bravado.

"A woman after my own heart," I reply, smiling up at her.

"I find *that* unlikely," she mutters, piquing my interest.

"So you never answered my question. Is there a husband? Wife? Significant other person?" I'm normally not this forward. I at least like to use a little charm and charisma to pull a woman in, but again, beer.

"Only if you count my rambunctious six-year-old boy and my ex-mother-in-law who lives with us?" Her eyes go soft at the mention of her son, and fuck if I don't feel it somewhere. *That explains the mother hen routine when she opened the door.*

"I'm sorry about the noise," I say quietly, my gaze dropping to her ruby-red lips, my tongue darting out to wet my own. I feel this weird draw to her. I can't explain it.

She dips her head, and my heartbeat goes crazy. I swear she's moving in for something... a kiss? Then drunken instinct wins out over well-thought-out logic. In other words, Jamie the dumbass makes an appearance.

I glide my fingers through her hair, close my eyes, and lean in to kiss her.

She freezes, her gasp causing my head to jerk back and my gaze to meet her wide, shocked eyes. Dropping my injured hand like a bomb, she scampers back until she's four feet away from me.

"What was *that?*" she exclaims, throwing an arm in the air. "I just wanted to *help* you, and you think that means I want to *kiss* you?" She leans in and points to the wall. "My *son* is asleep on the other side of that wall."

My mouth drops open, and there's a moment when I consider grabbing the offending hammer and knocking some sense into myself.

Before I can apologize, my phone starts vibrating on the floor.

"Keep pressure on that and if that's not your EMT brother on the phone, call him. And if you could keep the noise down a little, I'd really appreciate it. Some of us have to get up early," she snaps before spinning on her heels and crossing the room. She stops at the door, pausing for a moment before looking over her shoulder and adding, "and maybe invest in a first-aid kit, you know, in case drunken demo becomes a habit."

Then she disappears from sight quicker than a sinner at a church service.

I stare at the empty doorway she disappeared out of when the phone rattles again. After grabbing it, I answer the call and shove it in the crook of my shoulder, quickly pressing down on my hand again.

"Dude?" Jase asks by way of hello. My gaze is glued to the door as if I'm willing my Florence Nightingale wannabe to walk back through it. The throbbing pain in my hand is now the last thing on my mind.

"Hello? Are you there? You yelled then dropped the phone then all I heard was a woman's voice, so I hung up and called back. Are you okay?"

"Yeah… I mean, I slashed my palm open with the hammer."

"And you summoned up a guardian angel? Who was that?"

"Let's just say; I think I'm going to like this neighborhood a *whole* lot. Once I apologize for being an idiot and trying to kiss her."

"What?" he says with a laugh.

"Not my finest moment."

"Track her down tomorrow and say sorry for being a dick. Chicks love that shit."

"I'll take your word for it."

"Do that. I know what I'm talking about. How else do you think I've survived seven years with Natalie? I fuck up, I apologize with ice cream and orgasms, and all is forgotten," he says warmly. "Now tell me, is this neighbor hot?"

"Hmm," I reply, as I press my arm against the wall and lever myself back up to standing, the throb in my hand distracting me.

"She must be good to make you forget yourself."

"She's headstrong. Also rather forceful. She let herself in and went into full-on rescue mode."

"Niiice…"

"Feisty, too," I reply, a slow smile curving my lips.

"Oh…" he says slowly, his tone full of understanding. "Spunky is good. Sassy is better. But feisty, *oh yeah.*"

He's not wrong. Maybe I need a bit of feisty in my life. But first thing's first—I have to find the woman and apologize for being a right dick.

Then I'll get to know her a little better. It's the neighborly thing to do, after all.

Chapter Two

Jamie

I WAKE UP THE NEXT morning with a slightly sore head, a horrible taste in my mouth, and a throbbing hand. My brother Cohen swung by after I called him last night and dealt with my hand. He was annoyed when I refused to go to the emergency room, but even his EMT partner Cooper sides with me considering it was after ten.

But I don't have time to fuck around because today my brothers—Jaxon, Bryant, and Cohen—Jase, Matt, and my brother-in-law, Cade, are going to gut the entire interior.

After grabbing a quick shower and getting dressed, I swipe my keys from the kitchen counter and walk out of the house and towards my driveway. Once I'm in my truck, I look towards the house next door just in time to see the door swing open. Then I see her, my late-night savior, looking completely transformed. Long gone are the sloth pajamas and baggy tee. Now she's wearing dark blue scrubs covered with a zip-up jacket, but there's no hiding those sexy curves I caught last night. Her hair is pulled back in a ponytail, her face fully made-up.

Her son bounces as he walks by her side, hand firmly grasping hers as they disappear 'round the side of the house. I probably should've gotten out of the truck and talked to her, apologized for my behavior last night but maybe not in front of her son. That definitely wouldn't be the way to make a good second impression, especially since my first was so stellar.

If I hadn't seen and experienced her in her natural element last night, there's no way I'd even contemplate getting to know her.

I've never been intrigued by someone like this before, but there are more pressing matters to attend to. I'm not exactly geared up to let another woman distract me from my goal.

I start the engine and pull out, not wanting to be that creepy guy who sits in his vehicle watching people. I have coffee and donuts to collect, then a house to clear out. I'll think about my neighbor and how to make a good second impression later.

Later that afternoon, all of us guys are elbow deep in dust, drywall pieces, and destruction—the right kind—with the music playing at a respectable level. After all, I didn't think it would help my case to annoy the nameless neighbor any further.

Standing beside me, my brother-in-law Cade nudges my arm and jerks his head toward the table. "We've got an interloper, and he's not one of ours. Take a look," he whispers.

My eyes move to the table just in time to catch a small hand reaching out from under the table to grab a pizza box delivered thirty minutes earlier. I quickly think back to our conversation from the past few minutes, hoping like hell we've at least been semi-appropriate. The absolute last thing I need right now is another tête-à-tête with the mother of said hand about how I'm corrupting the poor boy's ears. Then again, we weren't to know we had an intruder sneaking in to pilfer our edible offerings. The hand disappears with a slice of pizza firmly in its grasp, and I grin.

Cade frowns. "What's that look for?"

I turn back towards him, holding out my hammer. "Hold this for me. The kid has just given me an opportunity I can't miss."

"Do I wanna know?" he says with a laugh, shaking his head. "You've got that look in your eye that can only mean one thing."

I lift a brow. "And what's that?"

"A woman."

I narrow my eyes. "What makes you say that?"

His gaze shifts over my shoulder and I instantly know the reason, because it's not only sisters who spread gossip—brothers do too—especially EMT ones. I dip my chin and groan.

"Cohen, did you forget to leave your purse at home today?" I ask, spinning around to glare at the tattletale. "Bet you told Mom, too."

"What kind of man do you take me for?" Cohen asks, sounding offended.

"A mama's boy," Jaxon and Bryant pipe up in unison, something they've been doing their entire lives. They give each other a high five while the rest of the guys chuckle, a small giggle from under the table catching my attention and reminding me of my new plan of attack. I had already decided on flowers and a bottle of wine after work one day this week, but since the opportunity to play the responsible neighbor has presented itself, there's no way I'm letting it pass by. Last night she got to help me. Tonight, I'm simply returning the favor.

"I'll be back," I murmur, slowly moving toward the table, spotting two little sock-clad feet sticking out from underneath. I decide a front-on approach is probably best. I'm not exactly a small guy, and scaring the dude is not what I want.

I drop down onto my hands and knees, the room going deathly quiet as I crawl under the table.

Lifting my head, I come face-to-face with our very own pizza burglar. "Hey, I know you…"

His big blue eyes go wide. His mouth drops open, but no words come out.

Scared that I've probably terrified the kid, I explain, "Your brother is the Hamburglar, right?"

His little face scrunches up in confusion. "I don't have a brother," he replies defiantly. "And I don't steal ham."

"I see…" I say, sitting on my butt and ducking my head down. Of all the things I've done in my life, tucking my six-foot-two frame beneath an old kitchen table wasn't exactly my best idea. "What about hamburgers?"

The kid's lips curve into a wry smile as he giggles again. "No."

I reach out and grab a slice of pie from the open pizza box, take a bite, and make a show of chewing and swallowing it down. "Damn, that's good."

"Mmhmm," he says, taking a bite of his own.

"Gotta drink?" I ask.

He shakes his head, and I grin at the ring of pizza sauce covering his lips.

"Damn." I slip my hand up to the table and reach out to grab one of the soda cans Bryant brought with him. I hold it out to the boy. "Want this one?"

He bites his lip, his eyes darting around as if there's someone else in the room he expects to tell him off.

"Hey. We've got more than enough," I say. He nods, slowly at first, then faster as his excitement starts to show. "Want me to crack it open for you?"

"Yes please."

I'll give it to the little guy; he's got manners. I figure his mom is a stickler for showing respect. Mine was the same with all five of us kids. *"Manners will get you far in life,"* she used to say. *"You can be an idiot, but if you do it with a please and thank you, people will let you be an idiot for a little longer."* One could never say my mom said the most flowery words of wisdom, but we knew her meaning was true.

"Mommy doesn't say damn. She says dang it," he informs me. He's pretty comfortable for a dude sitting in a stranger's living room aka demolition site, eating stolen pizza. I totally dig his attitude.

"We're guys though, right?" I say. "Guys can cuss when we're hanging out."

"Nuh-uh," he says, shaking his head. He takes a big slurp of soda from the can before releasing a long, loud belch that any grown man would be proud of. His eyes go wide as he covers his mouth. "Sorry, sir."

Yes, definitely a stickler for manners.

I can't help but chuckle. "You're fine. Say, what's your name? Because I don't think it's the pizza burglar?"

His eyes crinkle, and a smile appears. There's the cute six-year-old.

"Axel Rhodes Williams. My address is twenty-three Maple Street. My phone number is…"

I'm guessing this isn't his first rodeo at escaping his house, especially if he knows to recite his details when found/caught. I bite my lip and hold my arm out toward him, feeling encouraged when he slides his small palm against my giant one and attempts to shake my hand. "Hey, Axel, I'm Jamie John Cook, but you can just call me Jamie."

He pulls back his shoulders as if to try and seem bigger. "Hi, Jamie."

"Since you're not a burglar, I think we should blow this joint and go see what goodies you've got at twenty-three Maple. What do you say?"

"Yeah," he says quietly. "Hey, Jamie?"

"Yeah, Axel?"

"Can I take the soda with me?"

"Definitely, dude. Can we take the pizza too?" I whisper conspiratorially. He nods enthusiastically, and I bite back a laugh—what a cool kid.

I crawl out first, hitching a leg up and reaching my hand out for Axel. When we're both out from under the table and standing, we turn around to find six guys staring at us. My brothers are grinning, knowing that I can't resist a cute kid, and Jase and Matt just look dumbfounded. Cade shakes his head at me. Considering I dote on my almost one-year-old nephew, Harry, whenever I get the chance, he knows what I'm like.

"Guys, this is Axel."

"Hey, Axel," they say in unison.

"Axel, this is Cade, Jase, Jaxon, Bryant, Cohen, and Matt. They're all here to help me clear out the house. Axel here has assured me he's not a thief. I like to think of him as a hungry opportunist." Their smiles are unmistakable now as I continue. "However, we've decided to take our soda and pizza and make a break for it and check out the fridge at the neighbor's house."

"That sounds like an awesome idea," Cade says.

"Can I come?" Jaxon asks Axel, who looks my brother up and down.

"I don't think we've got enough food for two giants. Mommy hasn't been to the grocery store yet."

That makes everyone chuckle.

"Alright, guys. We're out. I'll bring back anything I find." I look down at Axel who is still holding my fingers. "You lead the way. I don't wanna get lost."

He grins up at me, clutching his soda in one hand and lets me go, grabbing the pizza box and struggling to hold it all.

"I'll take the pizza..." I lean down and take it from him and whisper, "...just in case we meet a pizza burglar."

His giggle is so infectious, and I'm smiling as we walk out the front door, down my front steps, along the sidewalk, and into Axel and the nameless neighbor's yard just as a car comes up behind us. We turn and see the gorgeous neighbor in the same outfit as this morning, stepping out of the vehicle.

Her eyes lock first on me and then drop to her son. She plants her feet and rests her hands on her hips. Then, in a voice only a mom can pull off, one that puts the fear of God into any child—young and old—she confirms my suspicions.

"Axel Rhodes Williams, what did you steal this time?"

And suddenly, her description of rambunctious makes all the sense in the world.

Chapter Three

April

THE LAST THING I EXPECTED to see when I pulled into my driveway was Jamie holding a pizza box, standing beside Axel in my front yard

Jamie—the drunk, irresponsible, infuriating, complete stranger I met less than twenty-four hours ago. The man who made a less-than-stellar first impression, now interacting with my easy-influenced son when said child should be inside and under the care of my ex-mother-in-law and lifesaver, Betty.

I park the car and shut off the engine, grabbing my purse from the passenger seat before stepping out. I watch Jamie as I walk toward them, moving my attention to my beautiful handful who takes an enthusiastic step toward me before freezing in place, the can of soda in his hand slowly shifting behind his back.

I plant my feet and lift my hands to my hips, quirking my brow at my now guilty-looking son. "Axel Rhodes Williams, what did you steal this time?"

He puts his little hands up and hilariously takes a step backward, said soda can dropping onto its side on the grass. Jamie looks down at the seemingly forgotten, most likely ill-gotten gains. His lips twitch as he watches my mini-me.

"Buddy, I think you might be in trouble," he whispers.

Axel's head snaps sideways and up. "Take me with you."

When Jamie shakes his head, Axel's cautious eyes return to mine.

Jamie shoots me a wink and if I was into tall, built, sexy guys wearing baseball caps, fitted tees, and worn jeans I really want to see from behind, then I'd almost swoon. Just the fact he wears his hair a little longer than short, has shoulders that would make a linebacker proud, with biceps that are more than a handful, has me thinking about very inappropriate things.

Lucky none of that does it for me. Who am I kidding?

"Hi, Mommy." He plasters a butter-wouldn't-melt, lash-batting expression on his face which falters as I narrow my eyes, tap my foot, and quirk my brow. I call it my triple-threat. Whenever I pull it out, Axel knows I mean business and soon stops all attempts to distract me from his behavior.

"Define stealing…" he says, tapping his finger on his chin as if deep in thought.

"Axel…"

We stand there in a silent stand-off, my son—who unfortunately inherited my stubborn streak—not flinching once as time starts to stretch.

"So, I might go," Jamie says, grabbing my attention. He turns to leave just as my front door opens. Our heads all swivel toward the new entrant in this meeting.

"Oh, *hello*," Betty says. Any other time, I'd be rolling my eyes at her sweet tone, mainly because I know exactly what it means, but I have an errant miscreant with boundary issues, and a stranger-neighbor who may have been wronged by said miscreant to deal with first. I can shut down any matchmaking plans she probably has later. Preferably with a glass of wine in hand and some of her renowned Bolognese inside of me.

Betty gingerly takes the few steps down to the yard and stops beside me. "Hi. I'm Betty. I'm the ex-mother-in-law who—"

My hand darts out to her arm to give what I hope Jamie sees as a seemingly reassuring squeeze, but that really is a shut-up-and-shut-up-*now* action.

Jamie rubs his palms on the front of his jeans, drawing my attention to his thick, muscular thighs, before holding out his hand to her. "Jamie Cook, ma'am. It's nice to meet you. I'm your new—"

"Neighbor. Yes. I've seen you from the window."

I bet she has. I fight against rolling my eyes. Don't get me wrong— Betty means well and has the biggest heart. There's also no way Axel and I would be where we are today without her. When push came to shove, she chose the two of us over her own son. It may be unconventional, but I love her just as much as my own mother.

"I'm sorry for any disruption I have or may cause." Jamie sneaks a glance my way before continuing. "Your daughter-in-law made it known the music was too loud last night, and I want to apologize for that."

Betty laughs her tinkly belly-laugh that is more endearing than aggravating as she waves him off. "Oh pfft. It was good background noise."

"If you're in a frat house," I mutter.

It's then that a certain menace spawn-of-my-loins puts out a huge— and rather dramatic—yawn, grabbing everyone's attention.

"I'm really tired, Mommy. I'm gonna go have a shower then get ready for dinner," Axel says, sounding super helpful and mature... except he's six, not sixteen, and there's only one reason my son—bless his cotton socks—is ever eager to have a shower and get cleaned up, and that is called guilt and self-preservation.

My hand shoots out to gently grab his bicep as he attempts to slip past me. "Hold up, bruiser. We've still got something to discuss, don't you think?"

"Not in front of Jamie, Mom," he says under his breath. His eyes are no longer calculating or planning—they're wide and pleading as he looks up at me.

I give a quick, curt nod. "Okay, Axel. How about you go inside with Gran, and we'll have a family meeting after dinner?"

He nods and holds his hand out for Betty. "C'mon, Gran," he says, before turning back over his shoulder. "Bye, Jamie. Thanks for letting me... uh... hang out with you."

Jamie grins down at him. "Any time, buddy," he says, holding out the pizza box to my son. "You're welcome any time." He reaches over and ruffles Axel's hair. Sneaking a glance my way, his fingers freeze when I shoot him a discreet headshake. "I mean, make sure you ask if it's okay first."

Axel beams up at his new friend. "Bye, Jamie. Say bye to the guys, and I promise I won't tell Mom you said I could curse," he yells from the porch.

"Shit... I mean..." Jamie stammers. I quirk a brow, my lips twitching as I watch the big, gorgeous—yet aggravating—man visibly squirming in front of me.

"Are you leading my sweet, innocent son astray, Jamie?" I ask softly.

His eyes narrow, the switch from guilty to smart-ass a physical transformation. He stands taller, his shoulders suddenly seeming broader, his smile lines deeper, and a dimple suddenly appears like a gift from the gods. *What in the world is this madness?*

"How was work?" he asks like we're the friendly kind of neighbors, ones who share coffee and cups of sugar, not ones who meet when I complain about the noise before stepping in to play nurse because he was never taught that boys plus beer plus demolition don't end well.

"It was fine..." I say, wondering what parallel universe I've stepped into.

"So about Axel. Don't be too hard on him. He must've snuck in after seeing the pizza being delivered. I found him under the table having a slice. No harm, no foul. I introduced myself. We had a chat. I suggested I bring him home so nobody would be worried about him."

"And the cursing?"

"Guys and power tools," he says with a shrug and turned up lips like that explains everything.

It does, but my little Houdini escaped again, and this time, he hid inside someone's house.

"Look, it's not a big deal. As I said, the guys and I weren't talking too much smack. It was actually tame considering my twin brothers can be rather loud at the best of times."

I visibly shudder at the thought of having *two* Axels. I love him to death, but easy is not his middle name. Axel Rhodes sounds similar to Axel Rose, and I should've known he would lead a life of hell-raising.

Jamie steps forward and reaches out his hand as if to rub my arm. "Hey, it's okay."

I need to make a quick escape to remove myself before I make a fool of myself or, equally possible; I throttle this man for being annoying and having dimples. It's time to redirect this conversation so I can go inside and get out of my scrubs. Then I can rewind and replay this conversation while over-analyzing it ten times. I'm such a chick.

"Well, I'm sorry if he bothered you. I'll replace anything he broke or stole, and I'll talk to him about respecting other people's privacy and property—*again*." That makes him chuckle, and I stand there with my mouth open like a carnival clown as I watch—and hear—his laugh. It's then that I reach up and figuratively slap myself. "Okay. Well, I have a son to feed and a mouth to educate."

Jamie shoves his hands in his pockets and rocks on his heels, his eyes glued to the ground as his shoulders shake with laughter. Then what I said and how it must've sounded registers in my head. *If he says one single thing about educating my—*

"Don't you hate it when you've got a mouth to educate?" he says, his lips twitching and his eyes dancing with amusement as they lift to mine. *Motherfucker.*

"Right," I scoff. "Says the guy who blasts rock music so loud it shakes my walls."

"It was nine o'clock on a Friday night!" he says, his volume rising just as fast as the red tinge of his face.

"I have a kid!" I say, stepping closer and reaching out to poke his chest.

"I didn't *know* that." His breathing is heavy now, the rapid rise and fall of my own chest matching his.

What a dick!

"You kiss your son with that mouth?"

Dammit, I must've said that out loud. A smarmy smirk transforms his face, and I immediately want to shut him up—with my mouth. Ugh! *Abort. Abort. Evacuate immediately.*

Thankfully, I'm saved by the bell—or Betty in this case—calling my name from inside the house.

I breathe a sigh of relief. "Well, this has been fun and all..."

"It's been something, alright," he mutters, his gaze dropping to my lips.

"On that we agree," I say, glaring at him. "See you 'round," I say, and I don't think I could sound any less enthused by the prospect.

"Is that a challenge?" he asks. *Fuck a duck. Pluck me with a feather. I'm done.* There's just something about the man that rubs me the wrong way in my head while my body wants him to rub me in an entirely different way, and that's something that's *never* gonna happen.

"Ugh, men!" I exclaim. I spin around and make my way toward my house.

"I'll try to keep the music down. Wouldn't want you to come over and let yourself in again," he retorts.

"Wouldn't want you thinking I want you to *kiss* me again," I grind out.

He snorts as he shuffles backward down my driveway, eyes locked with mine, lips curved up. "Doubt that's gonna happen anytime soon, sweetheart."

With that parting shot tempting me to commit violence, I quickly shut myself behind my front door. I lean back against it, trying to calm my racing heartbeat as my head threatens to explode at the sheer audacity of that man.

Construction and noise issues aside, I'm suddenly hit with the realization that my life is probably about to get a hell of a lot more complicated—and frustrating—as long as Jamie lives next door.

Chapter Four

Jamie

THANKFULLY, THE WOMAN WHO TURNS me inside out yet irritates me like no one else, makes herself scarce for the next week. She blows hot and cold worse than any other female I've ever met, and that's saying something considering I grew up in a house where us four brothers made our sister's life crazy.

We've made good progress on the interior demolition, and within days, we'll be ready to start construction. My skin is constantly dry; my hands often rough and cracked. I've never worked harder in my entire life yet I've also never felt so alive.

Standing in the shell of what is the physical representation of a life-long dream, all the sore muscles, early mornings, late nights and logistical nightmares encountered so far have all been worth it.

I'm living, breathing and sleeping this project. Now, more than ever, I'm one hundred percent sure that turning my life on its head to pursue this new venture was—and will turn out to be—the best decision I've ever made. For myself, my brothers, and my future wife and family. I have no doubt that achieving my own personal goals will help remove any lingering doubts put into my mind by my ex, Heather. Even the most confident of men can have insecurities, and what she did to me months ago definitely left a permanent dent in my armor.

That could be what rankles me so much about my still nameless-neighbor. Don't get me wrong; I have twice now seen sparks of interest in those blue eyes of hers, and I'm not denying that she's gorgeous, smart, and witty and that she has a body I'd willingly spend hours upon hours exploring. There's been more than a few moments this week when I've taken myself in hand and imagined she was naked in front of me, glaring at me in that unique way of hers that makes me hard. It's giving me ideas of ways I could turn that sass and spunk into feisty, fiery passion.

Tonight, however, is all about unwinding from a long, hard week with my brothers, and my best friend, Ezra Baker.

A car horn from my driveway announces Ez's arrival. I swipe my keys and wallet from the counter and shove them in my jeans pocket before walking out the front door and locking it behind me.

"You look like you need tonight," Ez states as soon as we pull out into the road.

I turn and lift a brow. "You could just say I look like shit," I say on a laugh.

"Well, I could, but that's not my style."

"That is true."

We fall into a comfortable silence until we reach the freeway on-ramp.

"So the neighbor?" he asks, merging into traffic.

I shake my head, my lips tipping up as I look over at him. "I thought vaginas were optional tonight."

"And he deflects."

"No. I'm avoiding the topic."

"Also known as deflecting."

"Wanna discuss your soon-to-be ex-wife marrying an ex-baller with a shit-ton of money, a Gold Coast penthouse, and a house in Miami?" I ask. He glances my way and smirks.

"So that's a no-go on talking about the neighbor," he concedes.

"Which one of the girls told you, Jax, Bry, or Co?"

"Your mother."

I drop my head back against the seat and groan. "God, that's all I need, my mother playing match-maker."

He reaches over and pats my knee before grabbing the gear shift again. "What's the worst that could happen?"

"Hang on. Why were you talking to Mom?"

"She was at Mom's place when I swung by earlier."

"I'm screwed then," I groan, dropping my head back against the seat and staring at the roof as if I expect to find help there. "Now they'll *both* be concocting a plan to have me married off by year's end."

"Better you than me," the bastard muses, making us both chuckle. "If it helps, I'm guessing I've only got a year at best before they turn their focus back on me. You know what they say…"

"Good boys need good wives so they can make us good grandchildren," we say in unison.

Our families have been close for nearly twenty-five years, ever since we moved in next door to each other. Ez with his two sisters, and us with the four boys and one girl, were forced upon each other by the moms within the month and from then on, it was always the Cooks and the Bakers—ironic, I know. We went together like bacon and eggs. Wherever one was, another was never far away. Between the two of us and my brothers, our sisters were tormented throughout their childhoods, and there's not a single guy in our high school who ever stood a chance at getting anywhere near first base with any of them.

"You'd think Abi and Cade having Harry would have satisfied your mom's need to nurture for the time being."

"It did, but he's one. Mom's getting the itch again."

"Damn, that means mine will too. Delilah's son is about to start school, and I doubt Faith is going to be doing the whole marriage and kids thing any time soon. She's not even seeing anyone."

Faith is Ezra's youngest sister who had the whole epic girl-next-door relationship with Bryant from age fourteen to twenty-two. Then something equally epic happened between them, and they broke up. Bryant came back from college in California and Faith didn't; neither one of them have ever explained what went down. As soon as Faith finished her doctorate at UC Davis, she hightailed it overseas and has been living in Australia ever since.

"So we're all back on the hook for procreating for the sheer purpose of keeping the moms happy?"

"Looks like it," Ez says with a smirk.

"And someone thought they'd throw me under the bus and tell Mom I might be next?"

"Not me. I wouldn't dare risk your vengeance. I'd say it was Jax or Abi; they're the biggest gossips amongst us."

"And speaking of Jax..." I murmur, spotting twin brother number one leaning against the trunk of his truck in the parking lot of our monthly Saturday local—a twenty-four-hour driving range.

"Want me to run him over?" Ezra asks.

"We probably shouldn't. Mom definitely wouldn't like that," I deadpan.

"You spoil all my fun," Ezra huffs. "It's not like she doesn't have another one of him."

"Three actually," Jaxon says as we park beside him. I roll my eyes at my smartass brother while Ezra just shakes his head. "What?" He leans his elbows against Ezra's open window. "I only caught the last of it, but I'm guessing Jamie is plotting my downfall again. Ez would never underestimate me." That just makes the two of us laugh at Jax.

I get out of the car and shut the door, Jax following me as I make my way to the back of his car.

"Did you remember to grab my clubs from Mom and Dad's?" I ask, leaning over the side to check.

"Nah, I went to pick up mine, saw yours, and decided you can just kick the balls."

"How 'bout I kick yours and then see who wins?" I say, flipping the bird just as the loud rumble of a Harley fills the air, Bryant slowly backing his pride and joy into a parking spot outside the facility's entrance.

"Where's Cohen?" I ask, pulling my clubs out. Hooking the strap over my shoulder, I move back to give Jax some room.

"Probably warming up so we don't all kick his ass again," Ez says with a shit-eating grin.

"Yo," Bryant says, putting his helmet inside the cab of the truck before moving around us and nearly jumping on my back. "Hey, old man," he says to me by way of greeting. I push him off and turn my head, grinning at him.

"Don't be mean. Ez is the old one. But it's not his fault. He can't help it if he's a thirty-five-year-old stuck in the body of a fifty-year-old."

"Assholes," Ez mutters, jostling Bryant with his shoulder as he walks past us. Jax holds out a set of clubs to his twin, who takes them off his hands.

"Let's go beat Cohen again," I suggest. "Can't have him thinking he might actually have a chance."

Ez chuckles. "The last time he kicked anyone's ass at golf—or in any capacity—was… let me think…"

"I vote for never," Bryant says with a wicked gleam in his eye. "But I think we should go show him how big boys do it."

"Don't lie, Bry. You still let Mom make your lunches."

"Only 'cause she works with me," he replies with a shrug.

"She works in the admissions office. You're on the other side of campus," I reply with a quirked brow.

"Look." Bryant sighs. "I can't help it if I'm her favorite."

Jax and I burst out laughing as all four of us make our way to the entrance. "You're so full of shit," Jax says, calling his twin out. "Mom told me you put in your sandwich order with her every day."

"You're just annoyed *you* didn't think of it first. I mean, at least I buy all the food for her to make it with. You just turn up and empty her fridge whenever you're hungry and in the area."

"And that's why he moved into a condo two blocks away. Then he's *always* in the area," I muse.

Gabe—the owner—waves us through when he sees us. "Cohen already paid for two hours. Go on up." Ez goes ahead to find our youngest brother.

"You deserve a raise, Gabe," I reply with a nod as I move to the stairs leading to the upper deck.

"I deserve a vacation—just me and the wife, and without teenagers determined to make life difficult," Gabe replies with a laugh.

Jax and Bryant chuckle behind me.

"Yeah. Our parents might *still* say that about us now," Jax adds.

"Let me know if you need more balls," Gabe calls out, *loudly*.

"Got enough already, Gabe, but your wife called and said you left them in her handbag this morning." Bryant waggles his brows, earning a grin and a muttered 'fuck off' from Gabe.

By the time all three of us reach the top deck, Cohen and Ez are deep in concentration, both of them taking time to perfect their swing like it's a golf major, not a driving range.

"Glad you got a head start, Cohen. Who knows when all that extra practice will eventually pay off?" Jax announces as we reach them, grinning widely when Cohen turns his head to scowl at him.

"You might finally beat Ez one day," Bryant adds.

Cohen just rolls his eyes and bends down to place another ball on the tee. He straightens and gets into position, looks down, pauses for a few seconds, swings his driver back, and hits the ball square on, sending it flying past the 150-yard mark.

Impressed, I blow out a low whistle. Cohen and I have always been close, and although I'm close to all four of my siblings, Cohen and I were always tightest. Maybe it's because Jax and Bry came out of the womb with that special bond twins have, or maybe it's because there's a seven-year-age gap between Cohen and me and I was always protecting him from the terrible twosome. Although it's probably more the fact that whereas the twins and Abi are rather extroverted and out there, Cohen and I have always been on the more intense, quiet, and brooding side of the spectrum.

In saying that, he's also the one brother who has *never* had any trouble getting ladies. I liken him to a quiet, unassuming predator who reels in its prey slowly but surely. He's always one to play the long game ending with a guaranteed win every single time.

"Are you guys gonna play catch-up or are you gonna sit there with your fingers up your asses and watch how a real man does it?" Cohen says, not even turning back to face us.

"Care to make it interesting?" I ask, taking the bait he so skillfully laid on us. *What did I say about unassuming?*

"Yeah, little brother, you gonna put your money where your smack-talking mouth is?" Bryant adds.

"Says the man who lost five hundred dollars to Jamie last month," Ez says, making me laugh. Bryant narrows his eyes before squaring his shoulders and making his way to a spare bay beside Ezra. Jax and I soon follow behind him.

"You asked for it," I say, puffing my chest out in fake bravado. I'm not as competitive as the rest of them. I come here to relax and catch up with the guys. Not losing and having to pay for dinner is a bonus.

"Loser pays for dinner," Cohen says, poking the bear just that little bit more.

"For the month," Jaxon adds.

Damn, now I really better win. If I don't, the house won't be finished in time to sell. "Let's leave it at that; otherwise you guys will be asking to cash out your investments, and there ain't no way that's gonna happen."

"Yes, *Dad,*" my three brothers reply before all five of us focus on the task at hand, and for the next hour and a half, we talk smack and take turns to whack golf balls out onto the lit-up grass, all of us pushing hard to get the most yards for bragging rights more than anything.

I should've known the fuckers were biding their time though, because before too long, Cohen breaks the ice. "So when do we get to meet the hot neighbor?"

Kill me now.

Ezra leaves me on the sidewalk outside the house around ten p.m., and just as I'm about to walk up the steps, I hear a car pull into the driveway next door. Curiosity gets the better of me, so I wait. When my nameless neighbor rounds the side of the house, she lets out a little squeak as I make my presence known.

I clear my throat. "Hey."

"Ah... hi..." she says, stopping at her front door. I walk to the edge of my porch, suddenly conscious that Axel and Betty are probably asleep.

"How was your night? Just finished work?" I ask stupidly, considering the light by her front door clearly shows me she's wearing the same blue scrubs she was in last weekend.

"Yeah. I've now finished the last of my twelve-hour shifts for the week."

"Damn. That must be hard."

"Tiring. Especially on a Saturday night," she says with a yawn. "How about you? Just getting in yourself? Or is hanging out on the porch the in thing these days?" Her voice is soft, and I realize it's the longest conversation we've had without sniping at each other.

"Just been at the driving range with my brothers and best friend. It's a thing we do every few weeks."

"Nice. That actually sounds quite fun."

My eyes widen. "You play golf?"

"No. I just mean hanging out with adults," she replies with a laugh. "Between work and Axel, I don't have much time for that sort of thing."

Interesting. I file that tidbit away for future reference. "Well I wouldn't exactly describe my brothers as adults most of the time, but I didn't lose our bet, so I wasn't the one paying for dinner."

She smiles. "That's a bonus then." She yawns again, the exhaustion written all over her face.

"I won't keep you, and I'll hold off on making any noise till after lunch, let you have a sleep in."

Her mouth drops open before she quickly catches herself. "Thank you. You don't have to do that, but I appreciate it nonetheless. Now I just have to hope Axel *lets* me sleep for a while in the morning before crawling into bed for cuddles and cartoons."

"Send him over here if you like. I'll just be sanding down the floors in one of the guest bedrooms."

"Oh." She waves me off. "You won't want a six-year-old hanging around while you're working."

I lean against the wall of the house. "Wouldn't have offered if I didn't mind. Honestly, any time he needs a little guy time, send him over. I'm sure he can help me out somehow. He seemed pretty content sitting under the table the other day."

"Stealing your food…"

"Well, there was that."

She studies me for a moment as if judging whether the offer is genuine.

"Anyway, I'll let you go and put your feet up since you've probably been on them all day. Just think about it. The offer is always there."

Her eyes soften, and she reaches for the door handle, almost as if to hold herself up. "Okay, I will. Good night."

I lift my arm and give her a short wave before pulling my keys out of my back pocket and moving toward my front door.

"Jamie?"

"Yeah?" I reply, turning my head toward her.

"Thank you," she says quietly. "He hasn't stopped talking about you and the guys all week. You might just help me make a little boy's day."

"Any time. I mean that."

She gifts me a tired smile before disappearing from sight.

I don't know why, but by the time I've walked inside the house and gotten myself into bed, I'm still smiling because I've given myself a new mission. Not only am I flipping a house and fulfilling my dream, I'm also going to make Axel's day whenever I can—and in doing so, make her life a bit easier, and hopefully make her happy with me for once.

Something tells me it won't be easy, but the feeling I got when that smile of hers—albeit tired—was shining on me will make it worth the effort.

Hopefully for the both of us.

It's only as I'm finally drifting off to sleep that I realize I still don't know her name.

I vow to change that as soon as possible.

Chapter Five

Jamie

TRUE TO MY WORD, I don't make a sound Sunday morning. To ensure that happens, I leave at the butt-crack of dawn and head over to Mom and Dad's house, knowing they'll both be up already and—if I'm lucky—I can kill two birds with one stone. First, I'll check it wasn't just beer talking last night and that Cohen really does want to help me with the floors today, and second, I'll score a free breakfast care of my loving mother who never lets any of her boys go hungry. That's probably why we're all more than six feet tall and built like Bears linebackers.

After giving a quick knock on the front door—a lesson I learned the hard way after walking in on my then empty-nester parents enjoying their freedom in ways a son never needs to see—I let myself in, seeing Mom halfway down the hallway, walking toward me.

"Did your nose lead the way?" she asks with a smile. I pull her into a hug, lifting her off her feet and making her laugh.

"Always with the bear hugs," she muses when I lower her to the ground again.

"Would you have it any other way?" I hook an arm around her shoulder as we move to the back of the house where the kitchen is.

"Not on your life," she replies. We turn the corner to find my father, Rick, and Cohen already at the kitchen table, coffees in hand, and plates full of food in front of them.

"Dammit," I mutter, jumping into action so I don't miss out. It can never be said that us Cook boys don't like our food. The rule of "first in, first served" has never been more true than it is in this house, and seeing Dad and my brother getting a head start on me, as well as half expecting the twins, if not Abi and Cade and their son to turn up at any moment, I decide to multitask: fill my plate while catching up with Dad and waiting for Cohen to emerge.

"Sleep in this morning, James?" Cohen asks with a cocky grin. The little shit calls me James to rile me up, a habit he's done since he was a dorky ten-year-old with an attitude.

"Says the guy who still lives with Mommy and Daddy."

"Hey, I only moved back so I could join the family business."

"Nothing at all to do with the home-cooked meals after a long shift, getting your laundry done, and the lack of rent to pay?" I tease.

He flips me the bird as Mom, Dad and I all chuckle.

"Leave your brother alone," Mom says. "He can't help it if he's a mama's boy at heart." Her lips twitch as she reaches over and ruffles Cohen's hair.

"Thanks, Mom. Nice to know you've always got my back."

"Well, it is nice to have someone else to get the blame for things occasionally," Dad jibes, his lips twitching as Mom gasps.

"Rick, take that back," she demands.

He pins her with a pointed stare. "Woman, I've loved you for thirty-six years and have lived with you for just as long. You know you blame me for everything."

"What else are husbands for?" she says, turning to wink at me.

Cohen and I both start choking on our food as Dad emits a low growl.

"Woman..." he rumbles. My brother and I just look at each other and roll our eyes, used to this kind of back and forth between the two of them.

"What?" Mom asks, sounding bored. "After this long, there's a fairly extensive list of pros and cons. Depending on the day or how much you're bugging me at the time, your usefulness rating varies." She finishes with a shrug and crunches some bacon in her mouth.

Those are fighting words, and true to form, whenever my dad is challenged, he fights back. Surging to his feet, he moves to where Mom is sitting, holds out his hand to her, pulling her up when she obliges, then dips down. In the blink of an eye, Mom is shrieking to be put down as Dad carries her over his shoulder, down the hall, and up the stairs, muttering, "I'll show you what I think about your damn pros and cons."

While all of this is happening, Cohen and I stand and lean over the table, piling whatever food we can onto our plates.

"Are you coming with me?" I ask, downing the contents of my coffee cup as he disappears into the kitchen for a second and comes back giving me a "duh" look.

"I'm not fucking staying here and getting scarred for life. We have an agreement. When I'm on shift, they can do whatever they want. When I'm here, it's hands off. So right now, I'd rather be any-fucking-where but here."

I nod because being the first born, I've been around my parents the longest, and when I say I've seen and heard things no child ever wants to hear, it's no exaggeration. "Let's get out of here then. We can bring the plates back later."

"Fine by me," he replies, halfway out the front door already.

When we reach my truck and hop inside, Cohen grabs hold of my plate and pulls out a roll of saran wrap from his pants.

"Dude?" I ask, my mouth dropping open at not only my brother's preparedness, but also considering just how hygienic this whole situation now is. To his credit, Cohen doesn't react. He just covers the plates before reaching over to put them both on the back seat.

He faces the windshield. I slowly drive down our parents' street while he puts his seatbelt on.

"So, why were you really there for breakfast?" he asks, playing with the stereo like it's his God-given right. Cohen may be the youngest, and he's definitely the quietest, brooding, and intense brother out of the four of us, but that's only around other people. When it's us boys, anything goes, like the country music now filling the truck.

I shoot him a side eye before shaking my head and turning down

Bryant's road. Since we forgot coffee, it looks like twin two is getting an early wakeup call too.

"I promised the nameless neighbor I'd keep the noise down till after lunch. I was hungry, and I was gonna see if you still wanted to help me with getting the floors prepped."

"Wait… you still don't know the neighbor's name?" He splutters before he bursts out laughing. "Oh God, this is priceless. Bryant is gonna have a field day with this."

I pull into said brother's driveway and put the car in park, spinning around to lean against the truck door and scowl at my baby brother with a death wish. "You *really* want to tell Bryant? I'm sure there are many things I know that you *really* don't want the twins knowing…"

"Like what?" he asks, his earlier amusement now somewhat tempered.

"I don't know," I say with a sly grin and a nonchalant shrug. "Are you willing to take the risk?"

"Fine," he huffs. "No need to get nasty."

"God, I love having leverage on you fuckers." I chuckle as I jump out of the truck and open the rear door to get my breakfast out. Cohen does the same.

After walking around the back of the truck, I meet up with him again, and we move towards the back of Bryant's house.

"So are you going to find out her name? I know we all give you shit, but you're not a man who mucks around when you're interested in someone."

My head jerks slightly. "Who says I'm interested?"

Cohen's look of "do you think I'm stupid?" says it all. I'm saved from answering when a half-asleep Bryant opens the door without a second glance, walking away from us with a muttered, "Just ask her out already, for fuck's sake."

Cohen and I face each other and start laughing as we cross the threshold and walk inside, breakfast in hand.

Before we can say anything, Bryant sticks his head out from the kitchen. "By the way, you fuckers better share that food with me, or else there will be hell to pay for waking me up before nine on a Sunday."

"Mom and Dad were—"

He holds up his hand, his skin going pale. "Enough said. Stay as long as you like."

In the end, we do share with him, and then we all sit on his couch and talk shop for a while before my phone buzzes on the coffee table with a text message from Dad. He writes just four words.

The coast is clear.

Well, thank God for that.

Later that day, Cohen and I have swung by the hardware store for supplies and are halfway through sanding the floorboards of the second bedroom when there's a knock on the door. After pulling my face mask off, I wipe my hands on my shorts and move down the hallway and across the now shell of what will be an open-plan living area to see who it is. Expecting it to be one of my siblings, I swing it open with a "Why didn't you just let yourself in?" to find my nameless neighbor and at her side, Axel. He's come prepared to help out, a toy tool belt on his hips and a plastic hard hat on his head.

Feeling it's pertinent to address my unexpected contractor for the day first, I grin at his mother before giving him my attention.

"You must be my new worker," I say, earning a wide, beaming smile.

"Yup. Mommy says you can't work without me and need my help."

I struggle to hold back my chuckle. I love that she made it all about him because the look of pride on his face is totally worth any shit she's given me in the past week. Not that I'm complaining. I'm not about to tell her that our little game of push and pull has been the most fun I've had in a while, or that a man like me loves the challenge a woman like her presents.

"Mommy says she needs to supervise me, and that I have to wear my hard hat at all times." He glances at his mother before looking back up at me. "Is it okay if she makes sure we do a good job?"

"Sure is," I reply. "You might get dirty though. Are you okay with that?"

He lets go of her hand and walks past me like he owns the place. "Oh, yeah. Mommy says I'm always getting messy. It's what boys do, and since you're a big boy, you must get dirty too."

It's totally wrong, but I can't stop myself from meeting his mom's now wide eyes. I wink at her, which earns me a quick scowl but also a gratifying blush, one that deepens when I sweep my gaze down her body and back up, liking what I see as I do. She's wearing a white tank with light blue bra straps peeking through, dark blue denim shorts that show a very nice amount of skin, and finished off with sneakers. By the time I reach her face again, she's biting her lip, which of course makes me focus on her mouth.

Needing a distraction, I look back down at Axel. It may be slightly underhanded, but needs must and all that. "Hey, buddy?"

"Yeah?" he replies, his chest puffing out a little as his fingers toy with the plastic hammer on his belt.

"No one's allowed on the building site without first giving their full name. Can you say it out loud for me?"

His mom snorts behind his back, but Axel's attention stays on me. "My name is Axel Rhodes Williams," he says proudly. I nod and hold out my hand.

"That's a strong name, Axel. You may enter the building site," I say, sweeping my arm out to welcome him in before straightening just as the nameless neighbor moves inside.

"Uh-uh, Mommy. You have to give your full name, or else you can't come in," Axel announces from my side.

She glances down at her son. "Mommy Williams?" Her eyes lift to mine, her brow quirking in a silent challenge.

"No, silly," he says with a high-pitched boyish giggle. "Your real name."

"Nurse Williams?" she says, shooting him a wink.

"Mommyyy…" he moans. "I've gotta get to work and help Jamie."

She looks at me, her glare meeting my amused one before she goes back to her son. "April Rose Williams. *Now* can I enter?"

Axel tugs on my hand and beams up at me. "Can she, Jamie?"

I tap my finger on my chin as if considering his request. "If you vouch for her, I think she can enter."

I turn and hold out my hand to his mother. I've always said that so much can be said without saying anything at all, and the moment April slips her hand in mine to shake it; I swear I see surprise, wonder, confusion, and a little edge of conflict in her gaze. I'm experiencing every one of those feelings too, as well as warmth, softness, and an overwhelming urge to do more than just shake her hand. *What do I even do with that?*

"Do I have permission to enter?" she says quietly, and even that has an effect on me. Needing to move this along before I do or say something completely stupid, I pull away and usher her in.

"Oooh, and Gran is baking muffins," Axel says, his entire body near-on bouncing with excitement. "She says I can have some if I work hard and build stuff."

"We should go do that then," I reply with a grin. "We wouldn't want you to miss out."

The little guy nods. "And if you work hard too, you could come and have a muffin with me."

April gets in before I can answer. "Axel, Jamie probably doesn't eat muffins when he's working."

"No, silly. This is after we've finished. He can come over, right, Mom?"

She reaches out and rubs his shoulder. "Jamie might be busy later."

"I like muffins," I say with a shrug. April's hand stills and her head snaps toward mine, her warring feelings on this development are plain to see. *Now I definitely want a muffin.* It's more than that though. I barely know this woman, but I do like to go toe-to-toe with her. She ignites something inside of me. I want to know who she is—outside of being a single mom living with her ex-mother-in-law. I want to get inside her head, discover what makes her tick.

"Hey, Jamie, who was it?" Cohen asks as he enters the room. "Oh hi… wait, don't I know you?"

She tilts her head and studies him. "I've seen you around the hospital. I work in the ER. You must be the EMT brother who had to make a house call last weekend," she says, sliding her eyes to me and lifting a brow.

Cohen laughs and walks over to us. "That would be me. You must be the caring neighbor. I've heard a lot about you," he replies, knowing exactly what he's doing.

"Is that right?" she says.

"Although he didn't know your name." The little shit has a smirk the size of Texas now. *Payback's a bitch, Co.*

"That's because I never gave it to him," she replies matter-of-factly. "Sometimes it's better to make a guy work for it."

My eyes narrow on her.

"You probably know our brother-in-law too, Cade Carsen?" Cohen asks. I groan and shake my head when she nods as both of them start laughing, Axel joining in too, although he probably has no idea what is so funny. *God, even Cade knows her.*

I shake my head and look down at my feet, my lips tugging up of their own volition. "Yeah, yeah. Keep it up, you two."

Cohen puts his arm on my shoulder and gives me a none-too-gentle squeeze. "Aww, James. All this time and Cade and I could've put you out of your misery."

"It's only been a week," I grumble, feeling somewhat sheepish, which is completely *not* me. Sliding my eyes to April, I catch her head tilted in what I've come to recognize is a habit of hers when she's trying to work something—or in this case, *someone*—out. And, not for the first time, I think it's fucking cute.

"Um, *hello*," Axel says, interrupting the now somewhat awkward conversation with me being the butt of the jokes. "Are we going to get to work? Things to build, muffins to eat. Remember, Jamie?" He puts both hands on his hips, looking every bit of the impatient kid he is.

"You're right, buddy. We don't have time for slackers like my brother, Cohen here, do we?"

"Nope," he says, accentuating the *P*. I nod, unable to stop grinning at him. He's such a cool kid; it must be near impossible for April not to bust a gut laughing at his antics.

"Follow me, Axel. It's time to get to work." I hold out my hand, and he quickly grabs onto my fingers. Just how much I like the sight of it hits me like a sledgehammer.

I upended my entire life to make this vision of mine—building a business, flipping houses, creating dream homes for people to make their own memories in—a reality in the hope that one day, I can do the exact same thing for myself. Part of that vision is a family, a partner who is proud of what I do and who supports me without question, and children of my own.

April and her rambunctious son have made me want that more than ever before.

And a quick glance at April's face as Cohen and I help Axel use the electric sander has me wanting one more thing—a chance to find out everything there is to know about April Rose Williams. Now I've just got to work out how to make that happen.

Chapter Six

April

I HAVEN'T BEEN OPPOSED TO dating since my ex-husband disappeared off the face of the earth five years ago, but between Axel, work, looking after Betty, and just life in general, it hasn't been at the top of my to-do list.

I'm not sure of the why or the how, but there's something about Jamie that intrigues me and makes me want to know more. He's so at ease around Axel, taking my little firecracker son and all his antics in his stride. It's shown me there's a different side to him than the single-carefree-guy-living-alone impression I first had.

Jamie is no longer the man next door who drives me crazy but also intrigues me. I mean, he is, but now there is a tangible connection there to people I know.

While I've worked with Dr. Cade Carsen for a while now—he even asked me out once back when he was a resident, and both of us weren't married—I've seen Jamie's brother Cohen around the ER quite a bit as well. He's friendly, a little standoffish, and all business normally, but he's a good guy.

And despite our head-to-heads, I know Jamie is good people as well. I wouldn't have brought Axel over this afternoon if I didn't think that.

Part of me can also admit that I didn't want to miss the opportunity to watch Jamie working with his hands—especially when the hot weather today had me hopeful he'd be wearing a wife-beater.

He didn't disappoint.

Seeing him look uneasy when Cohen and I were giving him shit was endearing. Here was this big man who looks like the Hulk and Wonder Woman's love child, almost blushing.

I honestly don't know what to do with this. Betty has already been in my ear about putting myself back out there, telling me in no uncertain terms that I'm not getting any younger—even though I'm only thirty-one—and making it clear that Axel can be the center of my world, but he shouldn't be the only thing in it.

But knowing that to be true and doing something about it are two different things. Then there's the fact that Jamie and I argue like cats and dogs, and of all the time we've spent together so far, 99 percent of it has had one—or both of us—annoyed at each other. That's not exactly conducive to considering dating the guy.

Hell, he might not even want to date me.

I'd date me though. I'm a catch. My lack of a social life—with the male species anyway—has nothing to do with confidence or a lack of self-esteem. It comes down to priorities and focus.

My priority has been Axel. My focus has been working and being the best mom I can be, making sure Axel is afforded every opportunity possible.

But now... a man has piqued my interest and got me thinking about everything I might be missing out on.

I wonder if we could go out to dinner and if he could keep his mouth shut...

"You look like you're trying to solve world hunger?" he says, startling me out of my thoughts. I turn toward his voice, my breath stuttering at the sight of a dirty, dusty and sweaty Jamie leaning on my fence, those well-worn work jeans of his hanging low on his hips, hugging his thighs. What sane woman finds a dirty, sweaty man sexy? *Me, apparently.*

Maybe I'm day-dreaming. It's Friday afternoon, and I've just woken up after sleeping off my night shift. I've only got one more to go before I have a twenty-four-hour shift change, then three days at work then a four day weekend.

"Did you work last night?" he asks, lifting the bottom of his T-shirt to wipe his face, giving me a glimpse of abs that tell me Jamie looks after himself, but he's not a gym rat. Another tick in the imaginary list of pros and cons for dating the neighbor.

He clears his throat, a light chuckle escaping his upturned lips as he totally catches me checking him out. *What on earth is wrong with me? Get it together, woman.*

I shake my head, hoping to clear the cobwebs from my brain. "I'm sorry. I've just woken up, and I've only got one coffee in me. I'm a bit... foggy," I explain, hoping my smile will distract him from the fact I'm completely and utterly mortified from him catching me checking him out.

His smile widens, and damn it; I swear I go a little starry-eyed. *Why won't the ground open up and swallow me whole?*

"Note to self: *April* takes a while to wake up in the mornings..." He lifts his wrist, giving it a shake to check his watch. *Yep, that's a quiver.* "And afternoons. Good to know."

"How's it all going?" I ask, nodding toward his house. "Betty says there's been lots of coming and going this week."

"Yeah. They're contractors from my friends' construction company. We're reconfiguring the interior floorplan and completely refitting the basement, so it's been a busy week."

"Wow. I'd be interested in seeing the finished product when it's all done."

His brows lift, and his eyes brighten. For a guy I mistook as being just another drunken single idiot when I met him, he seems to continually prove me wrong, like it's his mission to do so. "You thinking of doing work to yours too?"

I shrug by way of an answer. "Maybe, but I might wait until Axel moves past the age of destruction."

He laughs, soft and low. *And there's another mini quiver.* I really need to get out more if stomachs, wrist shakes and laughs are getting me off.

"He's a good kid, you know," Jamie says. My eyes widen, my head jerking slightly. He seems to read my reaction and quickly continues, "From what I've seen of him."

I giggle at his look of absolute fear as if he expects me to bite his head off. Firing-on-all-cylinders April might make him pay for that statement. Tired-from-four-night-shifts-in-a-row April can't really fault him for his observation. "He's a pretty cool kid."

"Definitely. He must get it from his mama."

I freeze, unable to process his compliment or work out the intention behind it. God, I wish I'd had more coffee, or... dammit. I look down, very belatedly realizing that yes, I did indeed walk out of my house wearing my sloth pajamas and a stretched-out baggy tee.

Twice now he's seen me in my pajamas and *not* for enjoyable reasons. Not that I'd wear this outfit if I had a man like Jamie anywhere near my bedroom. That would require a special trip to Victoria's Secret.

"Thank you," I say. "I'd say he's a mix of me and my ex, but I wouldn't wish that on Axel," I add a dry laugh to try and lessen the lead weight of that statement. It may be true, and I may have a little residual bitterness when it comes to the waste of space that was Patrick Williams, but a guy I might—if he wants to—date at some time in the future does *not* need to know that. I peek up through my lashes to find him leaning deeper into the fence, his forearms resting on the wood pailings.

"I sense there's a story there, but I might wait till you've had more sleep and more coffee before asking you about it." He doesn't sound like he thinks I'm a crazy ex, or as if he's trying to brush it off. His eyes are gentle as he watches me from across my lawn.

"Are you working tonight?" he asks, setting my heart to a slow gallop.

"Yeah. It's my last shift."

"Ah... okay," he says, looking up at the roof, then the sky, before hissing slowly through his teeth. He reaches a hand behind his neck, gripping it tightly. "Okay. I tell you what—I'm gonna check with Jase and see whether we can get a start on my roof shingle later tomorrow once you're awake, then we won't risk disturbing you."

I almost feel guilty, but his consideration makes my stomach do a little dance. "Sorry to be a pain."

He moves his head from side to side. "Not at all. You should never be inconvenienced..."

I shoot him a knowing smirk.

"...*again* because you had the misfortune of living next door to the house I decided to flip. It just means I need to be a bit more flexible with arrangements, so we don't cause any more hassle for you, Axel, and Betty."

"That's really thoughtful, Jamie."

"It's business," he says, matter-of-factly. "Let's call it community relations." His lips twitch as he fails to hold back a wide-mouthed smile. "Why do I seem to be grinning a lot whenever you or your son are around?" he asks, almost to himself.

I open my mouth to answer when an extremely handsome—and tall—man comes up behind Jamie and jumps on his back.

"Ugh," Jamie grunts, turning his head to look at his surprise piggy-back partner.

"Of course it's you," he says, chuckling as the man drops to his feet.

"And *you* must be the no-longer-nameless neighbor who—if you don't mind me saying—has impeccable taste in pants." The mystery man looks me up and down, turning to Jamie and bumping his shoulder. "Sloths, huh? You're *so* not living this down."

"Uh… hi," I say, stepping forward and holding my hand out. "I'm April."

He slides his palm against mine, and when our eyes lock, his grip flexes. He also doesn't let go. I catch Jamie's frown out of the corner of my eye, and I could almost swear I hear a low rumble in his chest.

That's when I see the unmistakable family resemblance. *This must be one of the brothers.*

"So which brother are you?" I ask with a giggle, finally pulling my arm free and crossing it over my chest.

"This is Jaxon," Jamie sighs. "He was dropped on his head as a baby and never quite got the memo about being tactful."

"Speak for yourself. At least I didn't miss the line for good looks or a big d—"

"Jax…" Jamie warns.

Jax drops his head back, exposing a rather nice-looking throat and bursts out laughing.

Jamie's dancing gaze meets mine. "I apologize for my brother's lack of class. I'd swear he was adopted if it wasn't for his twin Bryant actually being a semi-decent human—as far as my brothers go, anyway."

I shake my head, my thoughts going to their mom and how she must either have the patience of a saint or subscribe to a really good monthly wine box. What's worse, part of me wants to meet the woman to deliver *another* box of wine and to shake her hand. That makes four brothers and a sister I know of now. Five kids would drive me insane. I swear, I barely cope with just my one, and I have Betty's help.

"I think your mother deserves a medal," I remark.

Jamie nods. "Putting up with this one, I'd say you're right."

Jaxon laughs, and shoulder bumps Jamie once again. Unsurprisingly, Jamie doesn't even waver.

"I better go inside and help Axel with his homework before getting ready for work," I say to Jamie. I turn to Jaxon, who has the biggest grin on his face. "Nice to meet you, Jaxon. I think there's just your twin and your sister to meet now, and I'll be fully acquainted with the Cook siblings."

"You should come over for a family dinner. If you make it out alive, you'll be initiated into the inner sanctum for life."

My eyes widen, as do Jamie's. Jaxon laughs again and gives his brother a fist bump before walking back to the house and through the front door.

"I better get inside. Have a good night, and good luck with the roof tomorrow," I say.

"You too. And we'll try and keep the noise down."

I wave him off. "I sleep like the dead. I doubt anything will wake me but thank you." He nods, and we stand there staring at each other. His gaze does crazy things to my body. My nipples tingle, my skin ripples with goosebumps, and my stomach feels all too warm. When his smile turns into a smirk that I want to both kiss the shit out of and wipe off his face, I shake my head and spin on my heels, walking toward my front door.

"Bye," he calls out, and because I'm now all too aware that my pants are see-through in the light of day, I just wave over my head and near-on run into my house. "By the way—cute sloths."

I've never been one to get flustered around a man, but my cheeks are blazing by the time I get inside. I'm usually able to hold my own, and until today, I think I've done pretty well in going toe-to-toe with Jamie. But that's the second time I've seen him when we haven't argued. He saw me in my sloth pants—again—he didn't like his brother holding my hand, he's rearranging his contractors so they don't wake me up tomorrow, and he complimented me, not just on my son but on my parenting. There's *way* too much there to process, and a quick glance at the clock on the wall tells me I really don't have time to unbox all that just happened in my front yard... in my see-through pajamas... when I was half-asleep and semi-coherent.

This whole making-a-good-impression-on-him plan is going *so* well.

Chapter Seven

Jamie

ANY HEADWAY I'VE MADE WITH April slips away the moment I watch the ladder belonging to my roofing contractor slide sideways against the front of the house. I knew the guttering was sketchy at best, but it's like my life buffers to slow motion as the metal snags a bracket and steadily drags the rusted tube of aluminum with it before teetering on the corner of the roof. I hold my breath and offer a prayer to the building gods, knowing it was all in vain.

"Watch out!" one of the guys yells as not even a second later, everything comes crashing down, catching the fence between our two properties and smashing it into three broken pieces with an almighty bang. That's soon followed by another and another, the steady stream of shingle tumbling to the ground like a steady beat of a bass drum shaking the dirt and debris in a devastating continuous rhythm.

"Fuck!" another man yells when the old shingle finally stops falling. I look up to the sky, scrubbing my face, dollar signs flashing before my eyes. When footsteps bound down April's front steps, I wince as first Axel, followed closely by Betty, comes towards the destruction zone, both gazes snapping from the disaster to me.

"Oh no," Betty cries, her eyes returning to the formerly beautiful flowerbed now lying crumpled beneath jagged fence pailings topped with roof shingle and mangled guttering.

Axel doesn't hesitate to carefully make his way around the pile of waste to my side. I drop my chin to look down at him, his wide eyes and slowly upturned lips filling me with dread.

He points to a rose bush—in bloom, no less—and my gaze follows his finger. "Mommy planted that when our cat Missy went to heaven."

Direct hit to the fucking heart, kid. He either knows exactly what he's doing with the impromptu guilt trip, or his childhood ignorance knows no bounds. Any other kid and I'd go with the latter, but this is Axel we're talking about.

"And those hydray... hygray..." He looks to Betty. "What are they called, Gran?"

Betty's attention drifts to her grandson, her red-rimmed eyes a punch to the gut. *I have to make this right for April, and for Betty.*

"Hydrangeas, baby," she replies shakily, her hand lifting to cover her mouth as she takes the disaster in.

Axel grins. "Hydrangeas, that's right. Gran and I planted those last year for Mommy on Mother's Day. They made her smile."

I shake my head. "You're killing me here, smalls."

"I'm big. Mommy says so."

Speaking of his mother, a bleary-eyed—and still gorgeous—April appears in the doorway as if Axel's words have summoned her.

"Mommy," he shouts, jumping the trashed garden and running to her side. Her mouth drops open as she closes the distance between us, her eyes drifting to the roof where the two guys are sitting down watching this scene unfold, and then to me.

"I'm tired and grumpy so you'll have to forgive me for this, but WHAT THE HELL, JAMIE?" She yells, throwing her arms up in the air. "Is *this* what you meant by 'keeping it down?'" She even adds air quotes with her hands to make her point.

I step forward to cross over to their side of the fence—or I would, if there was still one standing—but stop dead in my tracks at the look of absolute fury she shoots my way. I know her anger is not all at me, but I feel it deep all the same. This is going to call for a big gesture to make it up to them—one that I'll need to call in reinforcements for.

"I'm so sorry, April. It was completely accidental and—"

"We're sorry too," Dave and Andy say in unison from above us.

Her eyes widen as she surveys the damage. "I just can't believe it. We'd worked so hard on this garden, and it was the first year all the flowers were in bloom." Her voice breaks and Axel leans up on his toes and wraps his arms around her hips. *Fuck.*

"It's okay, Mommy. Now we'll get a new fence *and* new flowers. Gran and I can fix this for you when you're at work."

Tears fall down her cheeks as she crouches down and pulls her son into her arms. She buries her face into his little neck and holds onto him tight.

"It's only a garden, I know," Betty says, moving toward me. "And I know I speak for April when I say we both know this was not your fault—"

"My contractors, my roof, my gutters, my fault," I say hoarsely, my eyes glued to April and Axel as they pull apart and smile at each other. "I'm going to make this right. I'll fix it all up, just as it was before."

Betty reaches out and pats my arm. "I'm not sure if that's possible, Jamie, but I do like your enthusiasm."

I meet her gaze. "Get April back to bed. I know she needs her sleep. I'll send the guys home and then get to work on making this right. I'm gonna need you to do a favor for me, though."

At that, I have her attention, and I formulate a plan to get all three of them out of the house tomorrow so I can—hopefully—break my back to repair what my roof broke. I also make sure to grab both her and April's mobile numbers, because they're going to be key to my success.

April straightens and takes one last wistful look at where her garden used to be before tangling her fingers with her son and walking back into her house with Betty.

Moving to untangle the ladder and help the guys off the roof, I take solace in the fact that I may have promised to fix the damage—as I am obliged to do—but deep down, I know it's not just about the garden. It's about showing all three of them I'm a man of my word, and that's something that means more to me than however much this project is going to cost.

With that motivation fueling me, as soon as Dave and Andy leave the site, my phone is to my ear as I call in reinforcements as I put all necessary plans in place for Operation Fix the Fuck-Up.

The rest of Saturday is spent putting everything in motion for the next day, and when I wake up first thing Sunday morning, I'm more determined than ever to make this right.

I receive a quick text from Betty at nine a.m. giving me a heads up that "Team Williams"—her words—is leaving in five minutes and will be out until late afternoon when she'll send me another text. Having the go-ahead, I send out my own group text, calling all of the pre-warned troops into action. Everyone—my brothers, Cade and Abi, Jase and Natalie, Matt and his wife, Mia, and my parents—is due to arrive as soon as they can with the supplies needed to get their pre-assigned jobs done.

The plan concocted last night between Jax, Bryant, Cohen, and myself is to get as much done as possible with what supplies we can get today, and to restore the garden and fence. With Betty's help, I was able to get the names of the plants and flowers that were there, and Mom and Dad are in charge of that side of things. *Who knew Mom's green thumb would come in handy so soon?*

With nothing more left to organize, I don some demolition gloves, lather myself in sunscreen, slide my well-worn Cubs cap on my head, and go outside to start clean-up. I'm joined by all three brothers twenty minutes later, Cade and Abi next, and Jase, Matt, and their wives a little after that, bringing with them all of the timber needed to replace the fence.

"So exactly how pissed was April when this all went down?" Jax asks when we stop for a brief lunch at the wives'—and my mom's—insistence. Jase, Matt, and their wives had to leave due to family commitments, but with the work we've all done this morning, there's no doubt in my mind we'll be able to get the garden and fence done in time.

"On a scale from normal level of irritation when I'm around to our sister losing her mind when you rearranged all the detachable limbs on her dolls as a kid? About a twenty," I reply, earning a gasp from our sister. My lips twitch when I turn to see her shooting a death stare in Jax's direction. When Cade wraps his arm around her shoulders and laughs—like the rest of the group—she glares at her husband.

"They had me believing it was a ghost warning me to stop annoying my brothers," she huffs.

Cade blows out a breath, shaking his head at the grinning twins.

"That's harsh." He still chuckles, pulling Abi in close and looking down at her. "But if Harry does that to any girls we might have, and if those girls are anything like you, I may just run away with him, purely for the preservation of the family line."

"Keep this up, and there won't be any family line, because Harry will be an only child due to his father never getting laid again," she warns with a dangerous glint in her eye.

Cade's head jerks up. "Well then, Jax and Bry, that wasn't very nice."

That just makes us laugh even more.

"The house is looking good, Jamie," Dad says, beaming with pride. "It's going to be a beauty when she's finished."

"That's the plan."

"And you're okay with living here while you do it?" he asks.

"It's good. I needed to do this. It was time to do what I've always wanted and this…" I say, waving my hand in the air, "…was a good project to start with. Relatively straightforward, a good redesign thanks to Ezra's plan, and with all of us boys chipping in, we'll be able to keep the labor costs down and turn a tidy profit to buy the next one."

"I always liked these bungalows. Our first house in Colorado had a similar layout. Your Uncle Keith and I renovated it ourselves just like you boys are doing. It meant your mother and I were able to sell it and get enough money to move to Chicago with all of you."

My throat tightens a little. I didn't know that, and hearing that this vocation is in my blood spurs me on. I was already pretty damn motivated to make this work—not just for me, but for my brothers— and this has just made me more determined to break my back and bleed myself dry to make it an absolute certainty.

"The pretty neighbor he's got his eye on helps too," Bryant says, earning a half-hearted scowl from me.

That gets Mom's attention. "At least you know her name now. You can't get to know a woman if you don't even know her name, Jamie. I mean, women do like that sort of thing."

"Did he tell you Cohen and Cade work with her?" Abi says with a giggle.

"She's definitely nice to look at," Jax adds, "and her son is hilarious." He then proceeds to regale the parents and Abi with the tale of Axel sneaking in during our demolition party.

I leave them to finish eating and take a bottle of water outside with me. Leaning on the porch railing, I survey how much there is left to do before April gets home. I try to imagine her reaction.

Will she be surprised? No doubt. Will she be happy? That's what I want more than anything. I may have only known her for a few short weeks, but every time we've interacted, I find myself more drawn to her, even when we end up going toe to toe. She's the kind of woman who works hard to provide for her family—something I've always wanted to do myself when the time comes—and despite setbacks that I want to find out about, she seems determined to make sure she, Betty, and Axel live their best life. I know that down to the bottom of my soul because it's evident in everything she does, the way she is with her son, and even the fact that she has her ex-mother-in-law living with them.

I just want to know everything there is to know about April Williams.

"You're doing the right thing, you know," Cohen says coming up beside me, mimicking my pose.

"Yeah. I just wonder at what cost."

"We have a contingency budget for any extra expenses. And Matt and Jase aren't charging us labor for the fence."

I turn my head, knowing I'm about to give my brother a lot more of myself than I normally do, but out of the five of us kids, it's always been the two of us who are the most alike in terms of personality. Whereas the twins and Abi could be—and sometimes still are—little shits, Cohen is more introverted.

I give a half-smile. "I'm not worried about that so much because I'll cover whatever extra we need."

"Jamie—"

"No," I say firmly. "I wanted this, I started it, and until we have a bigger surplus in the bank to back us up, I'll cover any shortfalls." He opens his mouth again, but I shut him down. "I'm not gonna change my mind about this."

He grins. "Yeah, I know. As long as you know we're not just in this with you. We're *in* this."

"And I appreciate that." I look back out to the garden and the fence that Jase and Matt built, now just needing a coat of paint and a final tidy-up. Then we need to put the last of the plants into the ground.

"So what did you mean about the cost then?" Cohen asks. Then the penny drops. "You like her."

It's Cohen—there's no point lying. He has always been able to read me like a book.

"Yeah. I hardly know her, and there's already a lot to like," I confess.

"She's not like your ex."

"Complete opposite."

"Then why are you worried?" he asks. "If I were a chick, I'd love this." He sweeps his hand out.

When I don't say anything, he continues. *Damn perceptive bastard.* "There's no way she'll think you did this to get in her pants. The April I know is not that kind of girl. She sees things for what they are, and that includes people trying to fix what they—or their contractors—may have accidentally broken."

My lips quirk up at that. "They kind of decimated it. You should've seen her face. Not only did we wake her after a night shift, but there were *so* many memories attached to her garden. Axel was telling me about every plant and the how, when, and why."

"And you felt that deep, didn't you?" he asks. *Damn sage.*

"It was a combination of things," I say, letting out a big sigh of relief. "She has what I want. She might even *be* what I want, and now that I'm working on myself to get to that place, I'm—"

"Scared?"

"Feeling cautious."

"Jamie, I've known you my whole life, and not once have I even thought of the word 'cautious' to describe you. That tells me she already means something to you."

"It's only been two weeks. We've spoken to each other four times."

"April is the kind of woman you can talk to for five minutes, and you will *always* remember it. She has a way about her."

"That's one description."

"And you'd call it?"

"Spunk."

That makes him laugh. "Fucking definitely."

"Are you two gonna do some work or are you too busy braiding hair and telling each other you're pretty?" Jax asks. He jumps down the front steps and walks around the lawn until he's standing directly below us.

"Aww Jaxon, you want to play with us? Are Bryant and Abi being mean to you?" I tease.

He flips us the bird as we both chuckle, the rest of the family soon coming outside behind him.

"You ready to get this done?" Dad asks as Cohen and I join them in the front yard.

"Yep." I look at my watch. "We've got about two hours before Betty said they'll be coming home."

"Well, let's get it done so you can impress the girl," Mom says with a huge grin, earning narrowed eyes from me.

"Mom…" I warn. She puts her hands in the air in surrender. "Okay, okay, I get it. Butt out, Mom."

I wrap my arm around her shoulder and press my lips against her temple. "Love you."

She snuggles into my side, tightening her hold on me and keeping me there. "Just promise me you won't ever compromise yourself and what you want for anyone."

"Never again," I murmur.

"Good," she says, stepping away and shooting me her best, most menacing mom look, and I laugh because April has mastered that exact same look with Axel. "Let's get to work."

"Aye, aye, Captain," we say in unison, resulting in all of us—including Mom—bursting out laughing.

Then we all do what she says: we get to work, and we get it done.

Chapter Eight

April

WHEN BETTY SUGGESTS WE HAVE a day out on Sunday, I welcome the change of scenery. I'm always a bit antsy, and—to be honest—grumpy after a long run of night shifts, and I knew that getting out into the sunlight and fresh air would do me good. It would also stop me from feeling guilty about how I reacted yesterday when Jamie's contractors accidentally destroyed the fence between our properties and leveled our flower garden.

I know I overreacted—it's a garden, for God's sake—but I was at the end of my tether and having been harshly woken from my much-needed sleep, I was a woman on a rampage, and Jamie bore the brunt of it.

I've made a vow to apologize for my behavior the next time I see him, but first there is my planned family day out with Axel.

However, after spending a few hours at Lincoln Park Zoo, then jumping on the train to get lunch in the city, I'm not the only one getting tired. But Betty is insistent that we keep going and Axel—although fading—is always easily led astray by his spritely grandmother.

The best thing to come out of my short-lived and disastrous marriage to Axel's father is my close relationship with his mother. When the number-one asshole of the century decided life was too hard and he needed an eighteen-year-old distraction, it was Betty who stepped in and told me what he was doing—gambling, drinking, sleeping with an almost-adult—and despite me being at home with our six-month-old baby, she helped me take control of my life again. She took Axel for the day while I changed the locks, packed everything that was Patrick's, and tracked him down at a seedy by-the-hour motel.

That was the last I saw of Patrick Williams. I never envisioned a life as a divorced single mom, but together, Betty and I have made a life for Axel to make sure he has a home full of love, stability, and consistency.

I love Betty as if she's my own blood and she returns that tenfold. For her to cut her son out of her life for her daughter-in-law and grandson, and never once waver or regret that decision, proving she's far stronger than I will ever be.

Grabbing a table at a much-loved Chicago eatery, Axel gives me his best puppy-dog eyes before launching himself at the chips and his Italian beef sandwich, a meal he's been eating for almost as long as he's been eating solids.

"So, Bets, it's time to spill," I say, watching with amusement as she takes a huge bite of beef, her eyes darting between Axel, the wall, the front door… to anywhere and anyone but me.

She knows I'm patient. I'm also like a dog with a bone, so until I get answers, I'm happy to sit here all day. There are salads and desserts, burgers and cakes. I can definitely wait.

I quirk a brow, watching with amusement as she puts her sandwich on the tray and wipes her mouth with a napkin.

"I wanted a nice day out. We deserve it," she says, definitely hedging.

I eye her suspiciously. "And that's all it is?"

"Gran just wanted us to do something nice, Mommy," Axel says, injecting himself into the conversation. I turn to him and smile, my heart melting.

I reach out and cover his hand with mine. "I know, baby."

We fall into a comfortable silence as we go back to eating.

Once we've finished and I'm reveling in my food coma, Betty speaks again. "That Jamie is a nice boy, isn't he?"

My eyes snap to hers.

"He's a big boy, Gran," Axel replies.

Betty's warm gaze goes to him. "He definitely is that," she says, looking over to me, a clear sparkle—and a suspicious glint—in her eyes.

"Betty..." I say, slowly

"What?" Her eyes widen. "I'm just saying he seems like a good man. He's great with Axel, and I may be out of his age bracket, but he's not hard on the eyes either." Then she waggles her eyebrows. *Matchmaker Betty is in the house.*

"He's okay, I suppose," I lie, and her answering grin is all knowing. She has always seen straight through me.

"And good with his hands..."

My mouth drops open, and she lets out a little giggle.

"He can build stuff and fix houses," Axel adds. "My friend Jamie is awesome."

Dammit, he's already won my son over. "He is, baby."

"And he has cool brothers," he continues

"I haven't met them," Betty says with a gentle smile

"They let me have their pizza and soda." Is he the Cook brother's head of promotion or something?

"And we talked about that, didn't we...?"

"Yep. Next time I'll knock on the door so Jamie can let me in, *then* I'll ask him before having pizza and soda." Axel's chest puffs out, and I can tell he's proud of himself. A giggle escapes me. This boy of mine is definitely one of a kind.

"What about you, April? What do *you* think of our handsome new neighbor?" Betty asks.

I shrug. "He seems like a nice guy."

"And...?"

I grin, knowing what she's trying to do but not yet willing to give her the satisfaction of acknowledging my growing interest in the guy. "And nothing. He seems to like destroying fences and corrupting my son." I try to keep a straight face when Betty gasps, but fail, earning me a scowl.

"I think you should get to know him," she adds. "What do you think, Axel?"

Ooh, now she's playing dirty.

"I'll take that under advisement," I mutter before turning my attention to Axel, hoping to change the subject. "Now eat your fries so we can head home."

"Oh no, not yet," Betty rushes out, looking at her watch. "I thought we could walk around for a bit. Let our lunch settle."

I tilt my head and narrow my eyes at her. "What's going on, Bets? And maybe you can start with the truth this time."

She sighs and looks to Axel who hilariously mimics her expression but adds a raised brow. "You tell her, Gran."

I jerk back, switching my gaze between the two of them.

"We wanted to surprise you," Axel explains.

"With ice cream," Betty says quickly. "We know how hard you work, and we thought ice cream might help."

"Help with what?"

"To make you happy, Mommy," Axel says, reaching out and tangling his little fingers with mine. *Little heartbreaker.*

I swear these two are up to something. Since I'll do anything to keep that smile on Axel's face, I decide to play along.

"I am happy, but I definitely think ice cream will make me happier. Let's go."

"Yay," he says, jumping up and knocking his chair back, making us laugh.

I decide to pause my interrogation of Betty until later. Something is definitely going on.

But first, it's time for ice cream with my now beaming son and his grandmother. I can't think of a better way to spend a Sunday afternoon.

By the time I pull the car into my driveway, my residual tiredness from my long week at work starts to kick in. After parking in the garage, we all get out, with Betty and Axel walking ahead.

I must've been in a daze when I drove in because as soon as I round the corner at the front of my house, I stop dead in my tracks at what I see. My white picket fence that just this morning lay destroyed against the broken flowers and flattened plants has been replaced, as has the garden, almost perfectly. I stare open-mouthed at my closed front door then back to the fence, and then beyond that to the smiling—my God, he's handsome—man leaning his elbows on his porch railing, eyes pointed my way. He looks cautious as if waiting for my reaction to what he's done.

No man has ever done something this thoughtful or meaningful for me before. Never in my life have I been speechless. It's like I've forgotten how to talk. My mind is so full of things I want to do and say, yet none of them seem big enough to convey just what I'm feeling.

The longer I stand there, the deeper his brows furrow, and it's his growing look of uncertainty that spurs me into action. I will my legs to move. The closer I get to the fence, the more I see just how much attention has been paid to replacing everything to look how it once did. *God, I was such a bitch to him yesterday.*

He straightens and walks down his steps and over toward me, stopping when he reaches the fence now separating us.

I swallow hard against the growing lump in my throat. "I don't know what to say except thank you. This is so much more than you had to do."

"No, it's everything that needed to be done."

I turn my head, taking my time to look along the entire length of the garden. "You got everything back where it should be."

"I pay attention when it's important."

My eyes lock with his, and I feel his words like a warm caress. What is it about this man that ignites a fire in my belly? And how do I explore this feeling without completely putting myself out there?

"If there's anything I've missed, just let me know, and I'll get it fixed tomorrow."

Tears prick my eyes. "It's perfect."

I get what today was about. He recruited Betty to help get me out of the house for the day so he could do all of this. "You and Betty—"

He nods and laughs, his lips twitching. "She sent me a text message on your way home and said you didn't make it easy on her."

"Let's just say she's a fan of yours," I reply.

He does a slow scan of me from head to toe and back again. "And what about you? Are you on Team Jamie?"

I study him. His arms are folded across his chest; his feet braced apart in a stance that screams *masculinity*. His black T-shirt hugs his biceps and shoulders, and his hair looks wet and tousled as if he's been running his hands through it.

Not only that, but this garden would have taken so much work. I wave my hand out. "After this stunt, I think I just might be."

"I might have to break things more often," he quips, and I burst out laughing.

"Don't you dare." I look over the garden again, memories of planting the flowers with Axel and Betty making me feel warm and fuzzy. I lift my head. "Thank you, Jamie. You have no idea what this means to me... to us."

"Yeah, I do. It's written all over your face, and it makes me feel good knowing I'm the one who put that expression there."

Oh fuck. Now he's being sweet.

I pop a hip. "Want me to throw some sass to get us back to our normal?" I say with a sly grin. His gaze drops to my mouth. When I bite my lip to try and stop myself from squirming, he groans, shaking his head and meeting my eyes again.

"So you like it then?" he asks. That small hint of vulnerability he shows me threatens to be my undoing. I'm drawn to confidence. I'm drawn to a strong and intense man. I even get off on back-and-forth banter with a smartass—often infuriating—man. But absolutely indisputable is the fact that a woman like me will forget any reservations she may have had the moment she gets a glimpse of a soft spot beneath that hard, cocky exterior, especially one who makes it his mission to surprise her with the sole aim of making her smile.

"Come for dinner," I blurt out, without analyzing the reason why I do it.

His lips curve into a lazy smile that any woman would walk over coals—or through her perfect new white-picket fence—to see every day for the rest of her life.

"Name the night, and I'm there, lovely."

My eyes widen at the endearment, and it settles around me like a soft, fluffy blanket.

"You're on," I reply. His eyes turn warm, and his grin widens, flustering me even more.

Right, I need to get out of here before I jump the fence and him.

"Mooooommmmyyyy..." I praise the lord for my son.

"Your master awaits," Jamie says with a laugh.

"I'll let you know about dinner."

"I look forward to it," he replies, his expression turning intense and hot, that soft fluffy blanket changing into a fiery inferno.

We stand there staring at each other, neither one of us saying a word, but that doesn't mean we're not communicating.

"Mom!"

"Right… um… yeah. I better go," I say, hiding my awkwardness by looking down at my feet. "See you 'round," I mutter before turning back toward the house.

"April," he calls out just as my hand reaches my front door.

"Yeah?"

"Glad you like the garden." Then he disappears out of sight and into his house.

As soon as I'm inside, Axel is at my side. "Mommy, did you see the garden and the fence?"

"I did, baby," I say, running my fingers through his hair.

"Jamie's awesome," he continues, full of awe.

I don't answer, but right now, I can't say he's wrong.

Chapter Nine

Jamie

I'M AT MOM AND DAD'S for dinner a few days later when I hear from April again.

April: Hi. It's April. I saw you weren't home, so I got your number from Betty. We wanted to invite you for dinner on Sunday if you were free.

Jamie: So I'm not the only one who's sneaky? I'd love to come for dinner. Should I bring anything?

April: I can be crafty when I need to be. Just bring yourself and a healthy appetite. I'm known to make a LOT of food.

Jamie: I come from a family of five men. It's eat first, or go hungry.

April: And I thought it was just six-year-olds who ate a lot.

Jamie: Axel will have nothing on me.

April: I'll make sure I stock up then.

Jamie: What time should I head on over?

April:	Maybe six? We'll eat early because it's a school night.
Jamie:	Sounds good.
April:	I'll let you go. Have a good night.
Jamie:	I'm just at my parents' for dinner. Seems they're not the only ones who take pity on the single man who sleeps on a mattress on the floor.
April:	You sleep on the floor?
Jamie:	There's no point moving in completely when I'm just going to be out again in a few months.

She doesn't reply again straight away, so I lift my head to meet the raised brows of my father and a knowing look from Mom.

"What?" I ask.

"You have a smile on your face," Mom says.

"I do smile, Mom."

"Not as much as you used to… when you were with—"

"It's fine, Mom. I'm just arranging dinner at the neighbors' house for Sunday. She invited me to say thank you for the garden."

Mom shrieks and claps her hands. "Did you hear that, Rick?" she says, elbow-bumping Dad and earning a grunt. "The big gesture got him the girl!"

"Good job, son. Women love that shit."

"Rick!" Mom's bump turns into a jab.

"Wow, woman. What was that for?"

I chuckle, earning a sharp look from Mom. "I haven't got the girl yet."

"But you want to?"

I sigh, knowing Mom will not let it go unless I give her something to go on. "I want to get to know her, yes."

"Good on you," Dad says. "Cohen says she's a good-looking girl, and she has a son she looks after by herself?"

Apparently, Dad is just as much of a gossip as Mom.

"With her ex-mother-in-law too," I say. Both of their heads jerk back.

"Sounds like there's a story there," Dad adds.

"That's just one of the many things I'm looking forward to finding out," I reply.

"Well if you need to build her another garden, let us know," Mom says, making me smile. "Oh, this is *so* exciting." She's literally bouncing in her chair. "We could have another grandchild sooner rather than later."

A strangled gasp escapes my throat. "Mom, I haven't even asked her out yet."

"Oh, I know. But a grandma can dream, can't she?" She pauses and tilts her head. "What does her son call her mother-in-law? I can't have the same nanna name as her; I'll need to be called something different. Harry is too young to call me anything, but I was going to be Grandma. Maybe it's not too late to change that."

I send Dad a pleading look, which he thankfully doesn't miss. "Marce, cool your jets. Besides, she might not even *want* to go out with him. She might shoot him down."

"Thanks for the vote of confidence, Dad," I say.

He just laughs and settles back down to watch the Cubs game on TV. "Anytime, son." His wide grin tells me he's totally talking out his ass.

I'm saved by another text.

April:	So this is an ongoing thing for you? Flipping houses?
Jamie:	Trying to make it into something, yeah.
April:	What did you do before that?
Jamie:	I was captain of a tourist boat.
April:	Whoa. I wasn't expecting that.
Jamie:	Ha ha. What did you expect?
April:	I'm not sure, but it definitely wasn't that.
Jamie:	What can I say? I'm full of surprises.
April:	I'm starting to see that.

Fuck that feels good.

Sunday can't come soon enough

><

Ten minutes after I've walked through April's front door, Betty's wide grin reminds me she only wants good things for her daughter-in-law, and the good thing she wants for her right now is me.

"Oh, Jamie, you're just in time," she says, ushering me inside.

I hand over a bottle of wine I bought—chosen with my sister, Abi's, recommendation—and follow her deeper into the house. It's the same original layout as my house, but definitely not in the same condition. Stopping in the open-plan living area, I can't help but admire the fresh paint and overall family feel. Its soft fabrics and neutral walls, with splashes of bold colors in the furnishings, give me ideas for staging the house when the flip is complete. I was going to ask Mom and Abi to help me with the interior design side of things.

"I bet our house is a bit different from yours right now," Betty says with a laugh. "Then again, we're a few years ahead of you."

I chuckle, grinning over at her. "Yeah, I'm aiming to do what you have done in three months."

"Some would say you're crazy."

"I like to think of myself as ambitious. Besides, I've got three brothers, friends, and contractors."

"That is very true," she says warmly. "Now, can I get you a beer before I con you into manning the grill for us?"

"Sure. I'd love one. Thank you. And no conning needed; I'm world famous in the world of grilling."

"World famous?" April asks, entering the room from the hallway as Betty leaves for the kitchen. If this house is the mirror image of mine, that would mean the master bedroom—provided that's where she sleeps—is on the other side of the wall to my room. *Damn, if that doesn't give me some ideas.*

I run my eyes down her body, taking in her light blue V-neck tee that hugs her curves and tight black jeans that almost look painted on. Her bare feet with red-painted toenails finish the relaxed-at-home vibe that I'm seriously digging right now.

When my gaze reaches her face again, I'm met with an amused smirk.

"You okay there, Jamie? Did you get your fill or should I walk out and come back in again?" She quirks a brow and shifts her weight to one side.

I open my mouth to tell her I'd be more than happy to take another look but I'm stopped by a running Axel slamming into my legs.

"You're here. I'm so excited," he says, jumping up and down. "Gran says I get to help you cook the meat on the grill. I *never* get to do that. That's man stuff, right?"

"I think you'll find girls can use a grill too, Axel," April says, laughing as she comes closer.

The boy spins around to look up at his mom. "I know. But Gran said that Jamie will teach me some tricks."

Her smile widens. "Okay. Well, why don't you go into the kitchen and get the stuff from Gran, and I'll show Jamie where the grill is."

"Right on." Then quick as the Flash on speed, he runs into the kitchen.

With Axel gone, it leaves the two of us standing there. There's that same fire in her eyes that I've found myself craving to see, but there's also a hint of trepidation, which is new. "Let me show you outside," she says, rubbing her hands on her thighs.

"Are you still okay with me being here? I'd understand if you—"

Her head snaps up. "Oh, shit. No—I mean—yes, I'm totally okay with you being here. I mean, I invited you, and Axel and Betty love you, and I—"

"Hey, lovely," I say, resting my hand on her arm, grabbing her attention. "Take a nice deep breath, then slowly let it out again."

I watch as her eyes widen before going soft, her chest rising steadily as she does exactly what I suggested.

"Now, before you find your feisty streak again..." I say, and her soft eyes turn alert and narrow. I forge ahead, closing the distance between us as I hope to both distract her and keep her—just a little—off-kilter. "You look fucking fantastic tonight, and you're lucky your son and Betty are here; otherwise this meal might have an entirely different outcome."

Her mouth drops open with a quiet gasp before I watch in avid fascination as she squares her shoulders, and that sass that I like so much snaps back into place.

She leans forward, deep into my personal space as I hold my ground. It makes no sense, but I swear, I like April in my face almost as much as

I like her nice and friendly.

"This is not a date," she hisses.

I dip my head, bringing us even closer, her warm breath fanning across my lips and giving me enjoyable scenarios to consider enacting in this impromptu—albeit goaded—stand-off.

"No, if this was a date, there would be wining and dining followed by a whole lot of other things that I'll leave you to think about for the rest of the night. Because while this may not be a date"—I fist my hands at my sides to stop from reaching out and pulling her hips against mine like every fiber in my being wants to do right now—"this is a precursor to one. Because there will be a date, there will be one-on-one time, and it *will* lead to us doing a whole lot of other things for you to think about."

Then I step back and swing out a hand. "After you…" I say. April's dazed expression turns to confused interest—although she could also be plotting my murder, so there's that. If that's the case though, I'll still take it as a win, because now I've planted the seed. If she's thinking of ways to end me, at least it means she's thinking about what I said.

"Jamie?" Axel says, running into the room and breaking the moment, and probably not too soon.

"Yeah, buddy?"

"We've got the hot dogs. Gran says you'll know how to grill because you're a big man with big hands, and when I'm a big man with big hands, I'll need to know too."

Betty comes up behind him, a beer bottle in one hand and barbecue utensils in the other. "If you take these, I'll leave you boys to it. April and I can finish off the rest of the food inside." She sends me a wink, and I catch April shaking her head at Betty.

"C'mon, Jamie," Axel says, near-on dragging me outside.

"This is the grill," he announces proudly. He places the packet of hot dogs on the table next to it before rubbing his chin and facing me. "Are you *sure* you know what you're doing?"

"Of course I fu—very well do…" I say, trying to cover my cursing. Axel narrows his eyes at me just the way his mother does—it's uncanny how similar it is—before yelling a quick "Wait there for a minute," and disappearing into the house.

I watch through the glass patio door as he runs into the kitchen, waves his arms in the air as he talks to April about something, then reaches into a cupboard and returns outside a few moments later with a jar in his hand.

"You waited," he says, sounding surprised.

"Where would I have gone? I'm not like Superman who can fly away," I reply with a laugh.

"Superman is *so* old. Marvel is better. Mommy says so. So does my friend, Adrian at school."

"Oh, really?" I say, nodding in agreement. I'm actually Switzerland when it comes to the whole DC versus Marvel debate, but Axel looks pretty into it, so I'll agree with whatever he says if it avoids arguments. If I want to date his mom, it probably pays not to alienate her son over fictional superheroes.

I switch on the grill while Axel places the jar he grabbed onto the outdoor table. "What's that, Ax?"

He tilts his head. "Am I not your buddy anymore?" he asks, his expression unreadable. The carefree Axel has left the building.

"Of course. Why do you ask?"

"You called me Ax. That's what Mommy and Gran call me. You always call me 'buddy.'"

"Sh—shoot. I better call you buddy then." That brings his smile back.

"Yay. So buddies give each other stuff, right?" he asks, reaching for the glass jar again and wrapping his little hands around it.

Unsure of where he's going with this, I decide to hedge my bets, nonchalant but also staying engaged and interested while I place the hotdogs on the heat. "As long as their moms are okay with it, I guess. What's up?"

He turns and holds out the jar for me, nodding down at it until I reach over and take it from him. "I wanted to give you this swear jar. Gran and I made it for Mommy, but she's given enough money to it, so I asked her, and she said it would be a *great* idea for me to give it to you… since you sometimes say bad words when you don't know I can hear you."

My head snaps up to meet April's dancing eyes through the glass. Both her and Betty are grinning like this is the funniest thing they've ever witnessed. If it had come from them, I might have been hell-bent on payback, but seeing the look of total sincerity in Axel's eyes, I know there is absolutely no mischief in this gesture.

"I would love to take this jar home with me, buddy," I say. "But you're going to have to tell me what the going rate for swear jars is. I haven't had one before."

He rubs his chin in what I'm now seeing is his "big boy, thinking face."

"I think one dollar a word would be fair," he says, nodding in agreement at his own curse rate. *Man, has inflation caused that or what?*

"Wow. That's a lot of money."

"Mommy says it means people won't wanna say curse words if they have to pay a lot for them."

I drop my head forward and laugh. He's so matter of fact. I actually wonder if he even has it in him to lie. "That's very true."

He looks to the sizzling grill then back to me. "Can I turn the hot dogs over now?"

"Sure thing, buddy. Let me show you how."

During dinner, our conversation is dominated by Axel telling me everything and anything there is to know about LEGO, planes, trains, cars, and school. He tries to get me to pick a side in the superhero debate; you name it, that kid covers it. The only time he is quiet is when he's shoving hot dogs and fries in his mouth and even then, us three adults take that time to also eat before preparing for the next deluge of questions. It is the most fun and relaxed dinner I've had in a long time. I can see just how much love there is in the house and just how much of an amazing mother April is. They have a good thing going on in this household—April and Betty are firm but fun, and man, they need a sense of humor with Axel around.

When April moves to take the dishes out, I stand beside her to help, as taught by my mother and completely ingrained in me.

"That's okay, Jamie. You're our guest. I'll just stack them on the counter and clean them in the morning," April says.

"Or we could do them now and get them out of the way..."

She meets my eyes. "Honestly, it's totally fine. I'll do it—"

"*But...*" I say, looking to Axel and Betty and winking, earning two amused giggles from our audience, "...why put off today what has to be done tomorrow?" I bite the inside of my lip and watch April's lips twitch.

"You do know you totally screwed that up?"

"Mommy! You owe the jar one dollar," Axel says, jumping from his seat and pointing at his mother in jubilation.

April's wide eyes go to her son before slowly narrowing on me. "You did that on purpose."

I shrug, unable to hold back a chuckle. "It worked though, didn't it? Besides, call it payback for me now owning the swear jar."

She doesn't even bother to deny whether she was, in fact, complicit in my adoption of said jar, especially since—if the past three weeks are anything to go by—she may well be the cause of my money going *in* said jar.

"Now are you going to let me help with the dishes?" I ask, earning a huff and a big sigh.

"Guess I don't have a choice then," she snaps half-heartedly. Betty grins at me and tilts her head for me to go.

I turn to Axel. "After I've finished cleaning up, will you show me your LEGO collection?"

"Yeah! Quick! Hurry!" he says, pointing to the kitchen like a prince ruling over his empire.

"Yes, sir," I say, taking the leftover dirty dishes and making my way to the kitchen where I find April standing by the sink. I place the dishes on the counter before moving to pick up a kitchen towel.

"Do you argue for the sake of arguing?" I ask, standing close behind her, my mouth by her ear, her heat radiating over my chest. "Or do you just like arguing with me?"

Her body leans toward me like she's my puppet and I'm holding the strings.

She turns her head, and our eyes lock. When her body touches mine, a jolt soars through me. The world around us seems to drop away as we stand there staring at each other. Then an excited shriek from the living room brings me back to reality. April stills before she moves forward, breaking the contact.

"Maybe you're just easy to fight with," she says. Her breathy tone makes it sound as if she's trying to be nonchalant—and failing.

I move aside and rest my hip against the counter, immediately feeling the loss of whatever just passed between us.

She doesn't look at me. What happened obviously took her by surprise. She lets out a sigh, shaking her head.

"Maybe you just like fighting with me," I say quietly. When I catch a wry smile curving her lips, I know I'm right.

"You're definitely easy to fight with," she says with a laugh as we go back to finish up the dishes.

"Nice play with the jar. That's an impressive switcheroo."

"I don't know what you're talking about."

"It's something the twins would probably do to one of us. Those two were the sneakiest sons of—"

"Watch it now," she teases. "You need your money for the house. You keep this up, you'll be stuck living next to us for a lot longer than planned because you'll be financing my son's college fund—or bail money—with your cursing."

"Can think of worse things," I mutter, just as Axel comes bounding into the kitchen like a kid at Christmas.

"Jamie," Axel says, coming right for me and reaching for my hand. "You've gotta come see my LEGO now. I made a plane, and it's *awesome*." His eyes are bright, and his little body almost vibrates with excitement.

April rubs her son's shoulder. "Ax, Jamie might want—"

"I'd love to. I've been waiting all night for you to show me," I say, earning a beaming grin from the boy.

April's lips part as her hand stills, her gaze meeting mine. "Are you sure?"

Axel tugs my hand, and I'm halfway out of the room before I look back and shoot her a wink. "Us boys have to stick together. Especially when LEGO is involved, right, buddy?"

"Right," he says, his chest puffing up. "Bye, Mommy."

I give a small wave as I walk backward, her soft expression reaching deep inside. I may be on my way to being the man I want to be, but maybe, with April, I could also be a man who builds himself up while building something entirely different—yet no less important—with his sexy, sassy, and spunky neighbor.

April walks me to the door thirty minutes later, having come to save me from a night of LEGO wars on Axel's floor. I probably would've been happy to stay there, but she insisted it was a school night and that "boys with big days tomorrow need their sleep."

With my assurance that I was one of those boys too, Axel said goodbye and made me promise to take the swear jar back home with me.

After stepping outside onto the front porch with me, April pulls the front door shut behind her, leaving us alone outside.

"Thank you for dinner. I had a great time. You've got a great family," I say genuinely.

"You're welcome. We may be a small unit with just the three of us, but we're definitely a tight one."

"And the swear jar is a good compulsory savings scheme... for me." I laugh, watching her do the same and finding myself absolutely mesmerized by it. "When's your next night off?"

Her head jerks. "Uh...Thursday..."

"Got any plans?" I ask vaguely.

"Nothing out of the ordinary..." Her bunched brows and confused expression are so adorable, I want to kiss them right off her face. But my mom always told us that good things come to those who wait.

"Want to have an unordinary one?"

"Is that even a word?" she asks, her lips twitching, her eyes light and bright.

"If it isn't, I'm making it one."

"Okay," she says slowly.

Unable to resist, I reach up and carefully hook a loose lock of hair behind her ear, gently brushing against the soft skin of her neck. I don't miss her slight tremble, and it makes me reconsider my decision not to kiss her now. A quick flash of movement from her front living room window in the corner of my eye serves as a reminder that we have an audience of one meddling, matchmaking Betty right now, and April might not appreciate putting on a show.

She tilts her head, her eyes roaming my face as if trying to get a read on me. "Jamie?"

"Yeah?"

"Are you asking me out?"

"Sure sounds like it," I reply quietly, unable to look away when my gaze locks with hers. Her breath catches, and again, I fight the urge to do something involving my hands, her hips, her mouth, and my arms around her back. My eyes drop to her lips, and I have to stifle a groan as her tongue dips out to wet them.

"Do you think that's a good idea?" she asks, her eyes gentle, her voice almost a whisper.

"Fuck yeah I do." There's no uncertainty in my voice. I don't want her to have any questions in regards to my determination when it comes to her. What strikes me most about this moment is that there's no sass, no spunk, no feisty comebacks, or smartass replies. This is April as her most honest, open self, and fuck if I don't like it just as much as when she's calling me out on my shit.

"Okay," she replies with a shrug. *A shrug.* Like it's just an everyday thing. Then she smiles, wielding it like a weapon.

I narrow my eyes, and her grin widens. "You're making me work for this, aren't you?"

"What can I say? I like it when a guy puts in a bit of effort to get what he wants." My self-restraint vanishes. I reach behind me, placing the swear jar on the porch railing, before turning back and stepping forward, closing the distance between us. She moves back and leans against the front of her house. I look to the left and see we're out of sight from the window. Putting an arm against the wall, I lean into her, resting my other hand gently on her hip and bringing my body in close to hers.

She tilts her head up as I dip mine, bringing our faces—and mouths—a whisper away from each other. A quiet gasp escapes her lips as the air between us turns electric. Visions of dropping my lips to hers and taking that taste I so desperately want flash through my mind.

"So Thursday?" I ask, my voice soft and low.

"Thursday. I guess I'll have to reschedule washing my hair." *There's the sass I've been missing.*

"I guess you will." I move in closer, gliding my cheek against hers and bringing my mouth to her ear. "But don't worry. I'll make sure that's the very last thing you think about on our date."

She runs her hand up my chest, hooking it around the back of my neck, so her mouth is against my skin before she whispers, "I'm gonna hold you to that," and she presses a barely-there kiss against the hinge of my jaw before releasing her hold on me.

I step back—a necessity to stop myself from taking this further.

Her lips curve into a sly smile. "By the way, that's three dollars you owe the swear jar."

"I'll put in a five and get myself in credit," I reply with a chuckle.

"Probably a good idea." My cheeks are starting to hurt from smiling so much, something that hasn't happened in a hell of a long time.

"Until Thursday, then." She nods and looks to the front door before returning her eyes to mine. "And try not to destroy anything *else* of mine before then. I'd hate to have to ream you out again."

"You never know," I say with a laugh. "But I'm starting to think you like telling me off."

She shakes her head. "And I'm starting to think you like it just as much."

Standing there, staring at each other, with me grinning like a loon. Needing to end this before I do something else we're probably both not ready for, I nod and take another step back. She moves off the wall, reaching for the swear jar and holding it out for me, turning toward her front door.

"Hey, April?" I say, looking back when I reach the bottom of her front stairs. She spins to face me, her hand resting on the door handle.

"Yeah?" Damn, that soft raspy voice of hers could be my undoing.

"You're welcome to call me on my shit any time you like if it ends with you agreeing to go out with me."

She laughs and shakes her head. "Good *night,* Jamie."

"Until Thursday…" I reply, flicking her a short wave before walking down her driveway, along the sidewalk and back to my house, swear jar in hand.

I've got four days to come up with a plan to make it count.

Four days until I get my chance to know April Williams, the mom, the nurse, and—most importantly—the woman. Because if she sets my body on fire the way she did tonight with just the touch of her lips to my cheek, then God only knows what she's gonna do to me when I finally get to kiss her the way I've been wanting to.

Thursday can't come quickly enough.

Chapter Ten

April

BEING WILLING TO DATE AND actually dating are two completely different things, and during a little freak-out on Monday night I realized I don't have anything date-worthy to wear in my wardrobe.

During my lunch break today, I came up with a plan of attack. If I'm going to give this thing with Jamie a real chance, I want to start it with a bang. Not literally. Having sex with Jamie on the first date would be way too much… wouldn't it? It has been a long time between drinks in that department, so I don't think I should rush into it. My vagina has probably shut up shop and put an "out of business" sign up by now anyway.

That brings me to now, finishing an hour early to rush to my favorite outlet mall to get the perfect date outfit.

Walking through the doors to the ER, I run chest-first into Dr. Cade Carsten and his equally—ridiculously—good-looking friend Dr. Noah Taylor.

"Shit, I'm so sorry," I rush out, finding both of them grinning at me. "Hi, sorry. Hi again."

"April, it's good to see you," Noah says. "I hear we now have a mutual friend?"

My lips twist up. "You mean Cade here? Yeah, we know each other."

Cade chuckles. "He's talking about my charming brother-in-law."

How much do they know and where are they going with this?

I eye them skeptically. Their expressions are both amused. "I know Jamie. He's my neighbor."

"And he's also been asking my wife for dating tips for Thursday night. Know anything about that?" Cade asks.

"Now that's a new one. I don't think we've had a situation where the guy has asked the girls for dating advice," Noah muses.

I shake my head at the two of them. "You guys are enjoying this, aren't you?"

"Not so much at your expense," Noah says.

"But definitely at Jamie's one," Cade says with a chuckle. "I've never seen the guy so nervous yet so absolutely focused on making sure he doesn't fu—I mean, screw—it up."

"That is kind of sweet, you know. Maybe you two should take pointers," I add, earning a laugh from both men.

"My wife hasn't got any complaints, but I'll take it under advisement," Noah says with a smirk that has no doubt dropped a lot of panties in the past.

"You'll have to come over sometime. Meet Abi and our son, Harry." Cade's offer takes me by surprise. I haven't even had a date with Jamie yet, and I've got the brother-in-law inviting me over to meet the sister and nephew already.

"Do all of you guys move at warp speed? Or is it just him?" I ask.

"It's just part of our charm." Cade grins. I just shake my head at both of them.

"I've gotta go. Places to be, clothes to buy," I say.

"Oh, date shopping. Abi is going to love this," Cade muses, pulling a phone from his pocket and typing out a text.

"I swear you turn into a woman more and more every day," Noah says, turning to Cade then back to me. "I better go too. I've got reports to finish before going home to remind my wife why she loves me."

"Good luck with that," I reply, waving him off. I turn back to Cade. "See you 'round?"

"Jamie is a really good guy. He's as genuine as they come," he says, his serious expression commanding my full attention, "and he has so much more to give to the right person."

"I can see that already, and we haven't even had a first date yet."

"I'm not going to tell you much more because part of the fun of dating is interrogating each other," he says. I giggle at that because he's so not wrong. "But Jamie is one of the best men I know, and I'm not just saying that because he's family. I wouldn't steer you wrong."

"I know. Thank you," I say, putting my hand on his forearm. "But I really have to go. Otherwise I'll be turning up to the date naked, and that's definitely not the kind of first-date impression a girl wants to make."

Cade's eyes widen before he bursts out laughing. "You should really meet my Abi. You guys are going to get on like a house on fire." He grins and moves toward the automatic doors for the ER. "Don't worry though. From what I hear, you could wear anything, and he'd be fine." He swipes his access card, then looks at me over his shoulder. "Even sloth pajamas."

The doors open and I'm left there, gaping at him as he laughs and disappears into the depths of the hospital.

I recover quickly, but now I've got a renewed focus on finding clothes to knock Jamie Cook off his feet on Thursday night because if he can't forget the sloths, I need to give him a sight that sears into his brain so deeply he won't remember anything else.

With that in mind, I walk to the staff car park and text my friend Ronnie who is set to be my shopping wing woman.

Operation Make Jamie Speechless is now in play, and I'm not going to stop until I leave that damn man speechless.

That's what you do on a first date, right?

Forty minutes later, I'm walking towards Ronnie who's at the front door of the mall.

"Babe, those scrubs…" she says, shaking her head.

"Hello to you too." I laugh as I give her a hug and hold her tight. "It's been too long," I say, letting her go.

"Work, more work. Oh yeah, then more work, and classes and exams." She sighs and shakes her head. "I know I wanted to go back to school and move forward and all, but being thirty and a student? Damn. So much work!"

Ronnie decided a year ago to go back to college and retrain to be a graphic designer. Despite her complaining, I know she loves it. She's now doing what she always wanted to, after having tried to toe her family's line for the first eleven years of her adult life. It was so amazing to see the weight that lifted off her shoulders when she finally gave up trying to make everyone else happy and chose herself for once.

"Well, we definitely miss having Aunty Ron around. Axel keeps asking when you're gonna go to Wrigley Field again."

"How is my little chestnut?" she asks as we make our way into the mall.

"Adorable, mischievous. A boy with my heart and his father's mind."

"So situation normal then?" She laughs, shaking her head.

Ronnie has been my bestie my entire life. Every single memory I have includes Veronica Nelson being at my side. She's my ride-or-die chick, and even when we do go a few weeks without seeing each other, it's like we were together just yesterday.

"Pretty much," I say with a giggle as we enter one of my favorite clothing stores.

Ronnie and I stand side by side, scanning the racks for anything that catches our eye. "Now, time for you to tell me about this new man." She looks over at me with an expression telling me she means business.

I blush, a coy smile playing on my lips. "His name is Jamie."

"Short for James or just Jamie?"

"His younger brother calls him James, but I'm not sure if it's just teasing or a thing they have."

"Interesting," she says, moving around to the rack opposite me. "So, c'mon, this is like pulling teeth."

"What do you want to know?"

"How did you meet?"

"I barged through his front door to complain about loud music and found him drunk on the floor with a split palm."

"Whoa. So, it's like his nurse fantasy came to life. Nice. No wonder he asked you out," she says with a snort. "He probably wants a naked reenactment."

"Ronnie!" I gasp. "We're going on one date. It may not lead to a second."

She levels me with a glare. "Chick, have you seen yourself? He's probably planned dates two through ten."

I shake my head, unable to stop myself from laughing under my breath. "Well, I'm only focusing on Thursday. We'll see what happens after that."

"Oh, just you wait. Once he sees you Thursday, there's no doubt what's gonna happen."

"Let's get on to that, shall we?" I lift a brow and usher her toward more clothes. I see a gorgeous black leather cropped jacket that I know will look fantastic with a shirt and jeans or a dress and strappy heels. I'm the queen of versatile wardrobe staples, so the jacket is a must-buy for me. It's clothes-lust at first sight.

Ronnie's gaze zeroes in on the same jacket. "Yes! You must get that, even if you save it till the date where you nail him. That jacket screams sexy MILF, and it will totally make him say 'wow.'"

I grin at her as I grab the jacket in my size. "I'd be happy with my boobs saying 'hi,' but wow is better."

"Exactly. Now don't even look at the price because I know you, and you probably haven't spent any money on yourself in maybe six months...?"

"Probably nine," I murmur under my breath.

"I heard that," she says with a half-hearted scowl. "That means we definitely need to find a dress to make your ass have its say too."

"Mustn't forget about the ass."

"Exactly." She slaps said derrière playfully. "Now, hand me your purse and try it on." I do as I'm told and when Ronnie's eyes light up with approval, I don't even need a mirror to know I'm getting it. "Now," she says, "let's go ring up the jacket, and then we'll go find the perfect dress to go with it. Oh, and shoes. We're absolutely getting shoes too."

"Guess I'll be putting my hand up for overtime," I mutter, but there's no bitterness. Ronnie's intentions are—and always will be—in my best interests. Together with Betty, she made sure I didn't spiral down into depression and lose my self-worth once Patrick and I ended things.

Once my card is swiped, and the jacket is wrapped, packed and in a bag hanging from my hand, Ronnie hooks her arm in mine, and like we're going to see the Wizard of Shopping, we skip out of one shop and into the next.

"You still haven't told me anything about Jamie other than he's a clumsy drunk who hurts himself, and that he has a younger brother."

"Three of them actually," I reply.

"And are they hot?" I smirk at her by way of an answer, and she sighs—loudly. "So Jamie, tell me about him."

"Jamie is good with his hands and good with Axel. He rebuilt my flower garden when his roofing contractors destroyed it. He can man a grill like he owns it, and he calls me lovely." I pause when she starts waving her hand in the air.

"I kind of hate you right now but I also *love* this for you too. So continue."

"He's hot, in a big, strong man way, has a voice like smooth, aged whiskey, and wraps his arms around me as if he's protecting me from the world while turning me inside out at the same time."

She levels me with a stare. "Can he kiss? Because even with all of that, if he can't kiss, it could be a deal-breaker."

"I don't know. We haven't kissed yet." Her mouth drops open as she stands there like a guppy fish waiting for food.

"You say he's hot without knowing if he can walk the walk? Jesus." She starts fanning herself, gesturing for me to stop. "I need a minute to get over the thought of that. I'm not going to get in on your action but if his brothers are single and anything like that, sign me up."

I bite my lip, trying to hold back a giggle. "Ron, I'll find out and let you know."

"It's your best-friend duty to look out for my interests: dating, sex, or all of the above," she says with a smirk.

"Right. Now that we've gotten past that discussion, we need to find something to go with the jacket," I say.

She scans the store and stops on a rack of dresses. "Let's split this task. You go to the shoe section and find a pair of grey, tan, or black strappy pumps. I'm finding you a dress."

"I need more than a dress. I need *the* dress, Ron."

She quirks a brow and tilts her head. "Have I ever led you astray?"

"Well..."

"College doesn't count," she adds with a wide grin.

"Then no."

"Exactly." She reaches over the clothes rack and wiggles her fingers at me, clasping my hand tight when I slide it in hers. "You deserve happiness, April, and if I can help guide you there in any capacity, you know I'm gonna be shoving you wherever you need to be. So go..." She gives my fingers a gentle squeeze. "Find some shoes that will have his tongue rolling out of his mouth and trying to find a home in yours, and I'll find the dress that'll have him dropping to his knees to worship you."

I grin, loving everything she's said and loving her even more. "I'd be happy with making him speechless... maybe throw him off his game for a bit."

"The man has game?" she asks, her lips curving into a knowing smile.

"He plays like he invented the goddamn game and he owns all the players."

"Okay," she says with a nod. "We definitely have to wow him now. And when he loses the ability to speak, you have my permission to thank me."

"It's a deal."

"The deal isn't done till you get laid, and I get to meet the brothers. But first, let's get you wowed."

Chapter Eleven

Jamie

AFTER A WEEK THAT HAS gone from bad to worse as far as the renovations go, the bright spot has been my date with April tonight. With contractor delays, tile order mishaps, and a case of the stomach flu knocking out workers left, right, and center, I need tonight to go well.

Now that I'm standing on her front porch, about to pick her up, I'm nervous as hell.

This is obviously not my first date, but it is my first with her, and this time it feels different. *She's* different. She's not afraid to go toe to toe with me, and she also doesn't take any of my shit. That has been refreshing and, weirdly, freeing. Even the day I walked into my old boss's office and handed in my letter of resignation pales in comparison.

I feel pressure every single day with this house project, but I've been using it to motivate me and inspire me to not only finish the flip early but also come in under budget. I have the aim of selling for a healthy profit to use for the next house, and the next one after that.

I'm pushing that all aside for tonight though because my sole focus is on April and showing her that this chemistry and electric dynamic between us is worth taking further. I want to know what makes her tick, and how she came to be a full-time working single mom living with her mother-in-law. I want to know what she likes and dislikes—other than arrogant neighbors who she takes a disliking to at first sight. I've been working to turn around that first impression of me, and after Sunday night, when I caught more than a glimpse of interest and definite attraction, I want to explore everything there is that makes her who she is.

In the seven months since Heather broke up with me, I haven't been open to dating anyone… until now.

With a bunch of flowers clutched tightly in my hand, I knock on April's door and stand there, shifting my weight from one foot to the other as I stare at the door, willing it to open.

When it does, I open my mouth to say hello but all thoughts escape my brain when I lock my gaze onto the absolutely stunning woman standing in front of me.

Her long brown hair that's normally tied up in a messy bun is now flowing over one shoulder, her eyes dark and smoky, her lips painted a subtle brown. I roam lower, drawn to the low V of her black dress peeking through a dark leather jacket that covers her shoulders.

Then there are her legs, which seem impossibly sun-kissed and long, finished off with the sexiest pair of tan strappy heels that I immediately imagine feeling as they dig into my ass.

She clears her throat, and I lazily glide my gaze back up to meet her amused eyes. "See something you like?" she asks with a quirked brow.

"Give me a minute. My brain has disengaged, and I need time to burn this image into my mind." *For later.* I do not say those last two words out loud. I was raised to be a gentleman after all.

Her smile widens, and I don't miss the tinge of pink tinting her cheeks. She looks down at my hand now strangling the flowers and back up again. "Are those for me?"

"Shit, yes… sorry." I clear my throat, shaking my head to clear the lust-fueled fog that's turned me into a bumbling idiot. If she wanted to throw me off my game with her outfit, she definitely won this round. I hold the bouquet out for her. "Yeah," I say quietly.

Her fingers brush mine as she takes the flowers from me, searing my skin in the process. "I'll just go put them in water," she says, shooting me a smile before turning and giving me a groan-inducing, fantasy-inspiring look at her outfit from behind. How long has it been since a woman has affected me like this?

She walks down the short hall and to a grinning Betty who gives me a wave. Axel comes racing into view, hugging his mom's legs. April bends down and gives him a kiss and a hug. He turns his head towards me and gives me a chin lift, of all things. Then April straightens, ruffles his hair, and hooks her purse over her shoulder. With her eyes locked with mine, she walks back toward me.

When she reaches my side, I hold out my hand, tangling my fingers with hers when her palm slides against mine, giving one last wave to Betty and Axel before closing the door behind us.

After walking her to my truck and closing the door behind her, I move around to the driver's side and hop in, concentrating on starting the engine and pulling out of the driveway. I don't concentrate on what I really want to do, which is go to my place and take my time showing her exactly how much I appreciate her outfit.

"You're quiet," she says once we're a safe distance away from home, reducing the temptation of ruining my plans to be a gentleman. "And you're gripping the steering wheel like your life depends on it."

When I lift a brow in her direction, she smiles as she looks back at the road. Knowing I need to give her an answer, I decide to go with the safe side of honest. "Honestly, driving is the only thing distracting me from how sexy you look tonight."

Her soft gasp is gratifying. "You don't look too bad yourself. Although I will say…" She reaches out and runs her index finger over the edge of my thigh, "…part of me misses those dirty work jeans you seem to live in."

That earns a chuckle, and I feel the tension seep out of me. "I promise I'll wear them on our next date."

Her eyes widen before her lips curve into a sexy smile. "Planning another date already? We haven't even finished the first."

"I'm an ambitious guy. What can I say?"

"Ambitious or cocky?"

"Maybe confident sounds better?" I reply, my lips twitching. I'm not sure I've smiled so much on a date before, and it's barely started.

When she doesn't say anything else, and comfortable silence stretches between us, I take that as a win.

"You didn't say no to a second date…"

She shakes her head and grins. "I'm taking it under advisement."

"I'll just have to win you over then," I reply with a smirk.

"Or maybe I just want to see the jeans again."

A growl escapes before I can stop myself. Reaching over the center console, I grab hold of her hand and lace her fingers with mine, and that's how we stay for the rest of the drive to my favorite Mexican hole-in-the-wall.

Twenty minutes later, we're being ushered toward the back of the restaurant to a booth I requested. I figured that the quieter it is, the easier it will be to get to know each other. Soon the server delivers our drinks—a margarita for April and a Corona for me—and we sit there like two kids on their own for the first time.

"This is weird, right?" she says, leaning towards me. We're sitting side by side, each framing a corner of the table, our calves touching underneath.

"It's good. I feel relaxed."

She laughs. "That's good. You seemed tense in the truck."

"I was nervous," I admit. "This week hasn't been good, and I've really been looking forward to tonight." Before I can overthink my instinct, I reach out and cover her hand with mine. Touching her feels so natural, how it's supposed to be. She doesn't blink an eye at the move; she simply turns her palm over and tangles her fingers with mine.

"So how's the house going? Is that the cause of your bad week? It always seems to be a hive of activity whenever I look over to your side."

I tense up. "Has it been disruptive? Because I'll talk to Jase, the site foreman if the contractors are causing any trouble." She gives my hand a gentle squeeze. "No, Jamie. I was just making conversation. Showing an interest," she adds with a wink.

"Shit," I say, letting out a breath. "Sorry. I'm just…"

"On edge?" she teases.

"Yeah. And scared of fucking up and saying something to piss you off."

She lifts her margarita glass to her lips, her eyes warm as she takes a sip and lowers it back to the table. "I've already decided you like me a little fiery. You seem to like riling me up so much, I'd almost say it gets you going." Those words roll off her tongue like an aphrodisiac. I'm not about to tell her she's wrong. "Besides, maybe I like you a little off your game. I like seeing there's a soft spot beneath that armor of yours."

That piques my interest. "Armor?"

"Oh yeah." She looks me up and down. "There's definitely a hard shell there needing to be cracked."

And just like that, she owns me.

"Enough of the heavy stuff. Tell me about Jamie Cook before he flipped houses."

I'm thrown a little bit by everything April says and does. She intrigues me, and the more time I spend with her, the more I want to know.

I take a swig of my beer and rest my shoulder against the side of the leather booth. "Left high school and always had an interest in boats, so I enlisted with the Coast Guard."

Her eyes widen. "Oh, wow. That sounds so cool."

"It was, but it was also draining towards the end. So, I finished my eight-year service, then got a job on a tourist charter boat."

She scrunches her nose up, looking adorably confused. "And now you flip houses?"

I can't help but grin across at her. "Yeah. I always wanted to start my own business in construction or carpentry, and I decided that in the current property market, I could really give it a shot."

"All by yourself?"

"I was going to go it alone, but my brothers wanted to get involved as well. So they all chipped in, and they help out whenever they can outside of their day jobs. I've always liked to make stuff, and I worked with my friends Jase and Matt on their construction site for a few months to learn the things I didn't know."

She leans back and lets out a breath. "That's so..."

"Dumb?"

"I was going to say brave. My friend Ronnie just made a dramatic career change, and from what I can see with her, it's a lot of work. I admire your ambition."

God, that feels so damn good to hear. "My parents have been a great sounding board; my whole family has. It's definitely hard work, but I can already see results from almost a month of work, so I can't wait to see how it looks when we're closer to the ninety-day mark."

"And the bonus of it all is you're helping to boost the property values of neighboring houses too," she says with a wide grin, holding her glass out to clink with my beer bottle. "So thanks for that."

"You're welcome… I hope."

"I have faith in you, Jamie. You seem like a man who goes after what he wants and doesn't stop until he achieves success."

This woman is good for a man's confidence.

The server arrives with our dishes, the two of us having previously decided on four different tapas plates to share between us: tamales, flautitas, nachos, and quesadillas.

"How about you?" I ask, after tasting what I've declared are the best flautitas in Illinois.

"I went to college and have been working at Northwestern ever since," she says with a shrug. "I love my job and being able to work the hours I do and with Betty's help, Axel gets to see his mom working hard for our future, and gets a stable, loving home in the process."

"I'm in awe of you. I know it can't be easy, but you should be very proud of what you've done and achieved. Axel may be… rambunctious… but he's a very cool kid."

Her eyes mist over, and her soft expression is begging to be kissed. But I could be projecting, because all I've wanted to do since I picked her up was kiss the living shit out of this woman.

"Thank you. He definitely keeps us on our toes," she replies.

I want to ask about her ex—Axel's father—and how he came to exit their lives, but that's not exactly first-date conversation material, so I table that for later.

I hold out the plate of nachos for her, and she spoons some onto her plate. From there, we fall into comfortable—safe—conversation topics. I tell her I'm originally from Colorado, how I love boats and want to own one in the future, and then about my brothers and sister.

She tells me about being an import from Michigan and how her parents are now retired and living in Florida. She likes reading and binge-watching TV shows and taking Axel for bike rides to local parks.

And, most importantly, they're a Cubs family. That definitely earns brownie points, and in my mind, I imagine taking April, Betty, and Axel to Wrigley Field for a game.

Her laugh is infectious, her smile addictive, and I find myself working for her smart quips and sexy smirks. I'm falling for the idea of being with her, and I can't wait to find out everything there is to know.

And, watching her for the millionth time tonight, I decide on a new goal: by the end of this date, I will taste her lips and feel her body close to mine.

Just a kiss—just having her close. What more could a man ask for?

Chapter Twelve

April

LACING HIS FINGERS WITH MINE, Jamie brings our joined hands between us. He dips his chin, and the brush of his lips against mine sends a tremor of warmth through me, centering in my chest.

"What did I do to ever deserve you?" He rumbles the words, and they vibrate against my skin.

I smile and pull back enough to meet his hooded gaze. "I guess I just have lower standards than you."

His eyes widen before he throws his head back and laughs, my attention riveted on the way his Adam's apple moves, how his shoulders shake, and the huge grin curving his mouth when he looks back at me.

"Can't argue with that," he says.

My smirk grows. "Well, there's a first."

His lips twitch as he shakes his head. "I'm far from complaining. Punching above my weight means I get to be here with you."

Inside, I'm swooning, but it's far too soon to show my hand. Jamie has not put a single foot wrong since knocking on my door earlier tonight, and for a man who's known for consistently riling me up for the sake of it, it's a surprising development.

"Good to know. Would hate for you to get a complex," I say. The longer we sit here staring at each other, the more the atmosphere changes between us, morphing from flirty to fierce and threatening to scorch us where we sit. We've kissed—well, not swallow-each-other-whole kissed. But when Jamie kissed me on my doorstep last week, my aggravation toward the man transformed into something entirely unexpected. Something I hadn't anticipated, and even sitting here on a first date with him, I'm still unsure as to what this is or what it has the potential to be.

Before I even have a chance to analyze anything, Jamie makes his move and in doing so, tells me without words exactly how he sees this going.

Crushing his chest to mine, he corners me against the plush red velvet seats of the booth we're in. His hand comes between us to cup my jaw, tilting it up, so we're eye to eye.

With our gazes locked, my heart beats faster and faster. There's a loud buzz in my head, blocking out everything except the two of us. In all my dating life—before and after my marriage—I've never felt such a powerful magnetic pull toward a man. Not with my high school sweetheart. Not with my ex-husband who was the man I thought I'd grow old with.

My at-first-aggravating, constantly antagonizing, and now completely contradictory neighbor is the one to knock me off my feet—figuratively—and throw all of my preconceived assumptions about him out the window.

He's taken me from not wanting or needing a man to dragging me headfirst into an all-consuming lust that has me wading in uncharted—yet not entirely unwanted—waters.

Something in my expression must change because his head stops mid-descent, his brows bunched together. "April, what just happened?"

I blink and stare at him. How can he read me so freaking well?

"Your face just went from soft and sexy to dazed and a little confused" He pulls back, resting his hands on my shoulders and giving me a little reassuring squeeze. "Whatever I did or said, please tell me."

I don't make him suffer because if this is to ever work, we have to communicate. I need to be able to tell him how I'm feeling. It's something my therapist drummed into me for the two years I saw them after Patrick left. "Do you ever think this seems too…"

His gaze warms, and my belly flutters. What is this man doing to me? He finishes my sentence. "Too… good? Right? Completely crazy but undeniable?"

"Easy," I whisper. His brows lift, before he relaxes, his eyes crinkling as his lips curve up.

"Easy is good," he says, like we're not having a rather unexpected—yet seemingly normal—come-to-Jesus moment.

"We bicker."

"Uh-huh." His smile widens. "And if I don't fuck this up, after tonight, we'll have new, thoroughly enjoyable ways to make up when we do fight. Or I annoy you. Or—"

"Maybe you should quit while you're ahead," I say dryly.

"Or maybe I like provoking—"

I close the distance between us and slam my mouth down on his, my fingers hooking around the back of his neck and holding him in place as I plunder his mouth. My tongue delves inside his parted lips like a heat-seeking missile.

I may have caught him by surprise, but a man like Jamie doesn't let an opportunity slip by, and merely half a second later, his arm snakes around my waist, his hand tangles in my hair, and our kiss turns into a kiss the likes of which I've never experienced before and probably will never experience again. The world around us ceases to exist. Every cell of my body, every sense still under my control is only focused on the man setting out to turn me inside out in the middle of this Mexican restaurant.

Feeling light-headed, I ease back, my cheeks hot, my breathing hard, my gaze locked on the blazing eyes of the man who just shifted my world off its axis.

He leans forward and presses his lips to the sensitive skin of my neck before pulling back. "You kiss like a wet dream," he rasps.

A startled laugh escapes me as my mouth drops open. "I what?"

"Oh yeah," he says, leaning into his elbow against the side of the booth, still staying close in a way I like far too much this early in a relationship. His smile brightens. "First time I met you and tried to kiss you, I knew you had some spunk. Just now, you grabbed me and used your lips to shut me up."

"I don't have spunk." I pull my shoulders back against the seat. He smirks, his eyes dancing with amusement. "I have sass," I reply indignantly.

"You have that too. But lots of spunk."

"Sass outranks spunk."

"You forgot feisty," he retorts, making me gasp.

I narrow my eyes at him, poking my finger into his chest. "You haven't even seen the start of my feisty, mister."

He leans in, his gaze lowering to the V of my dress before slowly raking back up to meet mine. I swear it's like his hands are gliding up and down my body and stripping me bare. "And I can't fucking wait."

Suffice to say, the rest of our dinner goes well. Soon, Jamie calls for the check, then—of course—we argue over my insistence to go halves. Once I win that battle of wills, he stands from the table and moves to my side, not once taking his eyes off me.

"Let's get out of here before I act on my impulse and get in trouble," he growls.

My nipples tighten, and I squirm in my seat at the thought of Jamie losing control. The dirty girl in me wants to see what happens when he does. She wants to go anywhere other than here so he can act on any damn impulse he wants.

But the responsible adult woman in me knows it's too much too soon.

"Maybe a walk along the shoreline might… do us good?" I suggest with a sly grin.

His eyes drop to my mouth, and his gaze narrows, his lips tipping up. "Yes. Fresh air. Let's go with that."

Instead of walking the three blocks to the lake, Jamie leads me in the opposite direction. When we arrive back at his truck, and he opens the passenger door for me, I wonder if he's changed his mind.

"I thought—"

I'm cut off by his hand hooking around the back of my neck and his lips slamming down on mine. I gasp into his mouth, and he takes advantage, his tongue delving inside. I can do nothing but melt against him as he presses me against the side of the truck, my hands grabbing hold of his arms and holding on for dear life while he pillages and plunders and I give as good as I get. I feel his hard body close to mine, and if we weren't standing in a parking lot in the middle of downtown, I'd entertain the idea of doing more than just making out because all of the build-up and tension snapping between us throughout the night has had me wet and willing.

He tears his lips from mine as we both suck in a desperately needed breath before he drops his gaze to my heels. "As much as I'd love to walk the lakefront with you, those shoes..." he says, gliding lazy eyes back to mine. His knowing smirk has my fingers flexing against his skin as a shudder courses through me.

"Let's take a rain check on the walk for another date," he says with absolute certainty, telling me there will be another time. His confidence in this thing between us is just as sexy as the heat reflecting back at me in his eyes. "But for now, let's go home."

His attention drops to my lips again, and I can't help but smile back at him. He glides his palms up my sides to cup my face in both hands, then dips down to brush his lips tenderly against mine. He slowly deepens the kiss, the gentleness so in contrast to before but affecting me just as much. This time when he pulls back, he rests his forehead against mine, our warm breath mingling together.

"I could get addicted to this..." He kisses me again, "...to this mouth."

With one last press of his lips to mine, he straightens and steps back. "We better go before I act on what I really want to do to you."

I push off the truck and lean my body against his. "We wouldn't want that now, would we?"

He drops his head back with a groan before shaking his head at me and holding out his hand, grabbing hold of mine, and helping me up into my seat.

He holds my hand the entire drive home, his thumb sliding back and forth over my knuckles, forcing me to cross my legs to help control the deep ache he's building inside of me. If his upturned lips and side glances are anything to go by, he definitely knows what he's doing and is enjoying the hell out of it.

When we arrive home, he pulls into my drive and gives me a warning look when I reach for the door handle.

"Let me do this." He lifts my hand to brush a kiss against my knuckles before letting me go and jumping out of the truck. Within moments, he's helping me down and walking me—again, hand in hand—to the front door.

Not wanting the night to end, I hesitate when we get there. He doesn't keep me waiting for long, guiding me backward and sideways until I'm leaning against the house and he's all I can see—all I want to see.

He leans in and rubs his nose against mine, inhaling as if to breathe me in. "You smell amazing."

I smile, pressing my lips to the stubble covering his jaw, his earthy cologne filling my senses. A soft sigh escapes me and his chest rumbles before he turns and captures my mouth, his tongue caressing mine in a slow, mind-bending kiss that leaves me wishing we were on his porch, inside his house, or that my hand was in his as he led me to his bed.

"I had a really good night," he says.

"Me too," I reply breathlessly.

"I want to do it again."

"Me too." I'm unable to think straight when he's this close, and I can feel every part of him against every part of me.

He lifts his head and looks down at me. "You're cute when you're flustered." His eyes are hooded and lazy. He looks so relaxed and happy, and I love that I'm the one who helped get him there. He straightens, and I grin.

"Don't worry. With our track record, I'll be argumentative and surly soon enough," I say.

"I like you feisty. I like you smiling. I definitely fucking love that look you get when I kiss you, and you can't stop touching me."

"Is that right?" I reply, my lips twitching. "You do know you're in trouble now that I know that."

One last press of his mouth to mine and he steps back, putting much-needed space between us to stop me from jumping him right here on my front porch. He reaches out and traces my bottom lip with the pad of his thumb, his gaze following it before lifting to meet mine.

"Sweet dreams, lovely," he murmurs, and with a brush of his lips on my cheek, he shoots me a sexy smile and lets me go, moving toward the driveway.

Watching him—and his magnificent ass—walk away, I can't wipe the stupid grin off my face or slow the fluttering butterflies in my stomach. I'm giddy, and when I'm lying in my bed fifteen minutes later, staring at the ceiling, my entire body is still buzzing.

Running through the events of the night, it hits me that never—not once—in my past has a man ever made me feel so wanted, so cherished, or so happy. And that's after only one date. I can't wait to see what else Jamie has up his sleeve, because if he's starting how he intends to carry on, I foresee a lot of dates—and more—in our future.

And I can't wait.

Chapter Thirteen

Jamie

EARLY FRIDAY MORNING, I'M SITTING with a coffee in hand at my favorite diner, a "ma and pa" kind of place where everyone in my family has been coming for years. It's good for breakfast or late-night snacks to sober up. A full-service eatery.

I'm waiting on Jason and Ezra to turn up for our weekly project meeting, and I'm still on a high from last night. The moment Ez walks through the door and spots me, his eyes brighten with a gleam that warns me I'm about to get grilled.

Sliding onto the chair opposite me, he clasps his hands on top of the table and smirks at me like the cat that got the cream.

No, that would be me, except I got April instead.

I look out for the waitress, waving her over. "My friend here would like to order us breakfast."

The waitress looks dumbfounded, and Ezra's mouth drops open, but he soon recovers. He plasters a charming grin on his face and orders two omelets with bacon, one plate of pancakes, and coffees for the three of us. Jase arrives just as the waitress is walking away, and he takes a seat next to me and places a notebook and pen on the table.

"Did you get me pancakes?" he asks Ez.

"Yes, I did, because you've been such a good boy," he replies sarcastically.

"No need to get snappy, my friend. Life is good." Jason is perpetually happy, and that's because he has a wife who is more than happy to serve all of his needs... multiple times. So, it's safe to say that Jason is always relaxed.

"How's it looking?" Jase asks, raising my suspicions. Considering he's the site foreman and he's just as up-to-date as I am on our progress, I'm sensing warning bells. The waitress returns with our coffees and disappears again.

I lean an elbow on the table and stare at Jase. "Is there something I should know about?"

"Building inspector caught something in the basement yesterday. I didn't want to say anything until I could get our engineer to have a look," he replies.

I close my eyes and take a deep breath. We have a contingency fund for unexpected expenses but hearing the words "basement" and "engineer" in the same sentence does not fill me with happiness.

"And what's the damage?" I ask, looking straight at him.

"It's not disastrous, but it's gonna hurt. Talked to Matt before I arrived just now, and the two of us can do it next week."

"And the cost?" I hold my breath and hope he doesn't make me wait long.

"Six to eight grand, tops. You can't really scrimp and save on something like this, and because it was the inspector who found it, no construction is allowed until he clears the repairs."

"He shut us down?" I grind out, my entire body tensing—both Jase and Ezra wince. Ezra opens his tablet case and brings up the house plans on screen.

"This is good," he says, studying the screen.

Even Jase frowns at that. "How can this be good?"

Ez looks up to meet my narrowed gaze. "Because it got caught early. You wouldn't want to have this issue crop up in a month's time once we've got all the drywall up and started all the finishing touches."

He's right—of course—but it still doesn't make it easy to hear.

"I guess that's what contingency funds are for?" I don't tell them it's up to me to cover any shortfall, but Ezra knows me well enough to assume. I'll take it out of my own pocket and reduce expenses elsewhere. I turn to Jase. "No work till Monday?"

"Jase and I will be on-site at seven thirty with our crew, and we'll get an early start."

"If it weren't so early in the morning, I'd be suggesting we move this to a bar," I reply dryly, half joking.

"Jamie, it's gonna be alright. You know these things can happen, and our guys like getting paid, so we'll just shuffle the work around to make it up. Matt agreed with me to not charge you for our time," Jase explains.

I open my mouth to argue, but he spears me with a "don't even start" glare.

"And you'll just owe us a favor or two. We know you're good for it, and we've had more than our fair share of roadblocks in the past. Let us do this and do it right," Jase says.

"Okay. So, the engineer has given you the specs?" Ezra asks, all business.

Jase nods. "Yeah, he did. We'll just need Jamie to sign off the cost of materials; then we'll be ready to go Monday."

"So, can I do anything this weekend?" I ask, dollar signs from lost time flashing in front of my eyes.

"Nothing classed as construction and nothing requiring power tools in the main dwelling. We can't risk any further movement in the basement."

"Okay... so that leaves painting the ceiling or landscaping?"

Jase and Ezra exchange a look. "Landscaping, sure," Jase says, "but you can't stay on-site."

"What?"

"You need to move out till the inspector clears us and lifts the stop order."

"Fuck!" I mutter, shaking my head and staring out the window over Ezra's shoulder. "Guess I'm staying with Mom and Dad then."

"You can if you want, but it's too far from site, and it'll mess with your head moving back home and dodging Marcy and Rick's 'arguments.' My guest room is yours for as long as you need it." Ezra to the rescue.

"Thanks."

Our food arrives, and thankfully, it serves as a much-needed distraction from the project woes.

"So how was your date?" Ezra waggles his brows at me over the top of the coffee cup perched against his lower lips.

"Date? What date?" Jase asks with his mouth full of pancakes. He thankfully swallows before continuing. "Who with?"

Ezra and his shit-eating grin get in before I do. "The neighbor."

"Wait, you know her name now?" Jase asks, his lips twitching.

Fuck, my friends are hilarious.

"Yes, it's April," I reply to Jase before turning to Ez. "And yes, the date was good."

"So, where'd you go?" Jase asks in a singsong voice. "And what base did you get to?"

My lips twitch, and it becomes impossible not to laugh at his idiot routine. "What are you, fourteen?"

He shrugs, shoveling more food into his mouth. I answer anyway, knowing Ezra will want to know too. "Dinner was good."

"You mean you didn't kill each other within the first thirty minutes?" he muses.

"No," I deadpan. "It was nice. We went to—"

"Let me guess—Mexican?" Ez says with a snort.

"What's wrong with Mexican? Better than your wife insisting you always go to the same Italian restaurant for the same Tiramisu every single time," Jase groans. I chuckle because Abi and her friends—including Jase's wife, Natalie—rave about that dessert every chance they get.

"So, you didn't kill each other. She made it home in one piece, and you seem to be intact. Does that mean it really did go well?" Ez asks.

I quirk a brow at my best friend. "You're doubting me?"

Ez holds one hand up in surrender. "No need to get defensive."

"With that kind of tension, I'm guessing the date didn't finish with a happy ending," Jase adds.

I shake my head. "Not all of us have a future wife who jumps us ten minutes into the first date."

Jase grins. "I'll have you know it was halfway through the first period of a Blackhawks game."

Ezra's mouth drops open as he stares in wonder at our site foreman. "Lucky fuck," he grumbles.

"My wife is one of a kind, my friend. She knew I was a catch the second she laid eyes on me."

"And has she had her eyes checked yet?"

I laugh at Ezra's retort, especially when Jase flips him the bird in response.

"When's the next date then?" Jase asks me, returning the conversation to April.

"I was thinking golf next weekend."

"With us guys?" Ezra asks, his eyes almost bugging out of his head. "But that's…"

"Such a cool idea," Jase says, nodding a bit too enthusiastically.

"Are you trying to scare her off?" Ezra splutters.

My head jerks back. "Fuck no. That's the last thing I want to happen."

"Honestly, Nat and I had a double date with Matt and Mia that first time, and now look at us," Jase says, beaming with newlywed happiness.

"I thought Matt and Mia didn't even like each other at that stage," I ask him with a raised brow.

Jase shakes his head. "Oh they didn't, but that's no different to you and April, right?"

I grab my coffee and take a long sip, both men's eyes watching me expectantly.

"You like her." That's Ezra, sounding impressed.

Jase leans back in his chair, eying me up and down. "Wonders will never cease."

"Thanks for the support," I snide.

"No, this is good." Ez smiles and nods, and now I'm even more confused at this weirdly happy side of him. "Who are you and what have you done with Ezra?"

Ez throws his head back and laughs. Then he hits me with the honesty stick. "You need a woman who keeps you on your toes and who isn't afraid to call you on your shit."

"My shit?" I ask, my brows almost reaching my hairline.

"Yeah. Guy shit. We all have it, and we need a woman who doesn't let us get away with it. That's when you know you've met the right one." Ezra's expression turns serious. "And we all know your ex was so not that."

"'She who won't be named,' you mean," Jase says with a laugh, adding air quotes.

We're all chuckling by the time the waitress returns with our bill.

"You can have this one," I say to Ezra, pushing the folder his way. "Call it payment for putting up with your smartass mouth."

"But that's not what you said about my mouth last night," he replies loudly.

"Ha fucking ha."

We walk along the sidewalk towards our vehicles, and stop at Ezra's car since it's the closest. "Do you really think golf is a bad idea?" I ask

"No," Jase answers immediately. "But I better go and get everything ordered for Monday." With a wave, he turns his back and walks down the sidewalk away from us.

Ezra leans against the roof of his car and studies me. "Do you *like her,* like her?"

"Yeah. Quite a lot actually. I know it's fast but—"

He nods. "I'd say no if you weren't sure about how you were feeling, but if you know this is going somewhere, then yes, bring her to golf."

My head jerks back, my brain hurting at the change of tack. "Really?"

"Would I steer you wrong?"

I laugh. "Well, there was that time—"

"I mean now, asshole." His smirk belies his words.

"Then no."

He opens his car door and lightly knocks his fist on the roof. "Then believe me. If you want April to know that you're a) in to her and b) see this going somewhere, then taking her to your boy's night out at the driving range will achieve that."

I nod, unable to argue with his logic.

"Let yourself in whenever you like. I'll be in the office till mid-afternoon, then I'll meet you at my place," Ez adds.

"No hot date?"

"You know I'd never step out on you, big daddy," he says, blowing me a kiss and disappearing into his car just as I burst out laughing.

They say you can't pick your family, but you can pick your friends. Ezra continues to prove that he was one of the best damn choices I ever made.

Chapter Fourteen

Jamie

Tuesday

April: Cohen gave me a weird look today when doing a patient handover. I couldn't work it out until he looked at my neck. Care to guess what he saw?

Jamie: Jamie can't come to the phone right now. Why? Because he's laughing too hard.

Jamie: Also, want me to beat him up? I don't need an excuse, but at least if you say yes, it's a good motive to tell Mom.

April: Or you can try and control your inner vampire next time you attack my neck against the back of your house.

Jamie: You attacked me first.

April: Tomatoes, tomahtoes...

Wednesday

April: Did the inspection go well?

Jamie: Yes! Thank God. Now I can move back in and forgo sleep to make up for lost time.

April: Let me know if you want some help. I've been known to be a killer when wielding a paintbrush.

Jamie: Thank you. Maybe you can come over and show me your skills ;)

April: Somehow, I don't think we're talking about painting.

Jamie: So, paintbrush wasn't a euphemism?

Thursday

April: I saw a really hot contractor walking into your house today. Do you know if he's single?

Jamie: I've heard you have a thing for men who work with their hands.

April: Yeah, my masseuse Pablo does amazing work with his hands and fingers. All over my body, in fact.

Jamie: Do I need to break down your door and prove to you just whose hands you should be thinking about?

April: Oh, I have been thinking about your hands too. Surprised you couldn't hear me through the wall last night.

Jamie: KILLING me here.

April: Oh, look, I have to get back to work. Talk soon.

Friday

Jamie: Would it be completely selfish of me to suggest you sneak over before work just so I can kiss you?

April: Kiss me or maul me? Because the difference between the two determines the likelihood of me escaping the house unnoticed.

Jamie: Can't you say you're coming over to help me with something?

April: Then your mini employee would insist he come over to help as well.

Jamie: I guess I can wait until our date tomorrow. Just know it's not my first choice. I'd much rather see you tonight.

April: I have to go in early to cover for a friend. The anticipation will do you good.

Jamie: The anticipation has been building since 2.5 seconds after I last saw you.

April: You can't say things like that when I'm about to have a shower. My hot water won't last as long as I need it to.

Jamie: Not helping, lovely.

April: I would help if I were there.

Jamie: I'm banging my head against the wall now.

April: Not as good as other banging, but don't hurt yourself. I have plans for you tomorrow night.

Jamie: See you tomorrow. If you find yourself wanting to come over earlier for a tour, I won't complain.

April: Duly noted.

Jamie: Have a good night at work.

April: Have a good night thinking about what you might get to do to me tomorrow ;)

The woman is wicked. She was right about anticipation, except for the fact it's now Saturday afternoon, and I already want to ditch our driving-range plans and stay in. I may not have furniture, a kitchen, or a proper bed, but I can make the rustic, minimalist look seem romantic, right?

However, as much as my body would love that, April is not going to be another notch on my bedpost. Not just because I don't technically *have* a bedpost right now, but because this thing between us is not just about the amazing chemistry we've got going on. I respect her. I'm of the impression that April hasn't given herself the time to get out there after her last relationship, let alone jump into bed with just anyone.

The respect she has for the life she's built, and the people important to her is admirable and inspiring because I too have the same values. Family is paramount, and the woman I want to spend my life with needs to believe the same thing. It's one of the reasons I want April to meet Ezra and my brothers. It should scare me, but I want Mom and Dad to meet her too, and for them to meet Axel and Betty. Almost five weeks and only one date, I already feel something for her, and you'd think after putting my trust and future plans in the wrong woman just seven months ago, I'd be running in the opposite direction of a relationship. Not this time. Not this woman. There's no way I can ignore just how *right* it feels when I touch her, when we talk, when I kiss her and taste her on my tongue.

I'm lost in thought when there's a knock at my door. A quick glance at my phone shows that it's too early to be April... unless she's come over for the "tour."

With a wicked smile, I move to the door and swing it open, coming face-to-face with a gorgeous-looking April in skin-tight, painted-on jeans... and a near-bouncing Axel with a container full of muffins in his hand.

"Hey, buddy. How are you today?"

"I'm good. I heard Mommy tell Gran she was coming for a tour of the house so I asked if I could bring my boss some of her muffins." He holds up the container, and I take it out of his hands.

"Thank you, Axel. The boss would love a muffin." I tilt my head and eye him suspiciously. His proud grin is contagious. "But I always share with my workers, and lucky for you," I say, making a show of looking over my shoulder at the empty room, "you're the only worker here. Do you know what that means?"

"More for me," he shrieks, grabbing the muffins and running past me and into the house. April steps forward to come in, but knowing I probably have five seconds to get what I want, I wrap my hand around the edge of the door, closing it behind me enough to block us from Axel's view. April's eyes soften when I close the distance between us, run my fingers through the loose hair at her temple, and slide them down to the back of her neck, then dip my mouth to brush gently against hers.

"So, this is a group tour now?" I whisper.

She slowly opens her eyes, her lips twitching with amusement. "Could you turn down that cute little face? He totally knows what he's doing to me when he pulls the puppy-dog look."

My mouth quirks up. "Would that work for me?"

She runs her hand down my chest, around my hip and lower, grabbing my ass. "Maybe, but just knowing you're around and that I get to do *this*"—she flexes her fingers, tightening her grip and definitely getting my cock interested—"makes me putty in your hands."

I steal one last kiss before pressing my lips to the hinge of her jaw. "When you're in my hands, the *last* thing I'm going to be thinking about is putty."

"Guys! Are you coming in or what?" Axel calls out from inside.

"My dictator awaits," she says quietly, her eyes hooded and focused on my mouth. "But I reserve the right to continue this discussion later." She glides her hands back to her side before squeezing her body against mine achingly slowly as she passes by me to get into the house.

"You bet your ass you will," I mutter, stepping back and closing the door.

After two muffins—Axel made me—I give them both a tour of the house and the progress we've made so far before leading them outside and explaining the plans for the garage and backyard.

Two hours later

April and I walk into the driving range hand in hand. If the wide eyes of Gabe behind the counter as I pay our fees are anything to go by, the boys aren't going to make this night easy for me. Then again, I've known those fuckers their whole lives and Ezra almost as long, so I would never have expected anything less.

Gabe doesn't say a word though—just hands me my receipt and wishes us both a good night. A few minutes later, we emerge out of the stairwell onto the upper deck—the only level we play on—and I spot the guys straight away.

"They're gonna give me shit," I say as we walk towards the guys.

"I like them already," she replies.

"They'll probably give you shit, too."

"Still don't see the problem."

"They're almost as protective of me as I am of them."

"And that's one of my favorite qualities of yours."

That literally stops me in my tracks. I tug on her arm as I turn to face her, pulling her hard against my body. She must read my intention because this time she initiates the kiss. It's not a respectable peck though; she dives straight on in there, lifting up on her toes and crashing her lips against mine.

"Get a room," Jaxon yells out.

"You should charge tickets for that." That was definitely Bryant.

"Where's my video camera?" That one I'm not too sure about.

I lift my head to see April grinning up at me, her hand moving around to rub her thumb over my bottom lip. She goes to step back, but I tighten my grip on her waist, holding her in place. She quirks a brow, a flex of my pelvis earning a knowing smirk.

"Oh," she whispers.

I shoot her a sardonic smile. "Mmhmm," I say, my gaze narrowing when she starts giggling.

She tries to wriggle from my grasp. "I was just going to—"

"You're gonna stay here until I'm at least half-mast. I won't live it down otherwise.

She tilts her head. "And you think standing here with my girl bits against your hard boy bits is going to help your situation?" She bites her lip, and it takes every ounce of control not to kiss her and bite that lip myself.

A minute later, I've willed myself down so that certain things are *not* as obvious, and we finish the short walk to where Ezra and my brothers have set themselves up, April struggling and failing to stop giggling at my predicament.

"You're so gonna pay for that," I mutter under my breath

"That's what I'm banking on."

"Hey, old man. Where did you pick up this teenager?" Jax says, coming up to us and shaking my hand. "If she likes Cook men, she might like a younger model," he adds suggestively. A growl vibrates in my chest, but Jax ignores me.

"He told me he had twin brothers," April says, taking his hand and shaking it, then jerking back when he goes to lift it to his mouth. "Jamie has told me so much about you."

Jaxon's head rocks back, his eyes wide. "He has?"

"You're Bryant, right? Your brother can't stop saying how you're his favorite. He said Jax was a cocky little shit who would probably try and steal me away."

I have never seen Jaxon speechless... until right now. April being April, she struggles to hold a straight face, and I look down just in time to see her lose it, a giggle escaping her lips when she does. I pull her into my side and kiss her quickly when she tilts her head my way.

"Brilliant," I say.

"You mean that's *not* Bryant? Oh no," she says, dramatically feigning regret.

"I always knew I was his favorite," the real Bryant muses, stepping forward and shoulder-bumping Jax out of the way. "I'm Bryant. Excuse Jax, he suffered in the womb because of the size of his ego."

"The size of something anyway," Jax mutters, grinning.

With my palm pressed to her lower back, I urge April forward to a smiling Ezra as Cohen steps up to take his shot, probably because he's trying to get a head start on the rest of us but also because he's the one brother who already knows her—before me, in fact.

"This is my best friend, Ezra. Ez, this is—"

"The woman who has dazzled our Jamie," he says, landing me in it. *Why did I think this was a good idea again?*

"He's dazzled by me, is he?" she says with a giggle, rubbing her fingers up and down over my hip. It's such a reassuring, intimate gesture that's just for us, that I really couldn't care less what shit the guys try to pull tonight. I'm the one with April on my arm, and that's where she'll stay if I have anything to do with it.

She grins up at me before returning her gaze to Ez. "That's good to know because he's kind of made a good impression on me too."

"Kind of?" Ezra asks with a laugh.

"Yeah. He's also good at getting under my skin, so I guess I'm happy with dazzling him in return."

"Now that we've all met her, do you think we can make tonight's bet so we can see if she can hit a ball?" Cohen asks, coming toward us with a smirk before pulling April in for a hug.

He leaves his arm hanging loosely around her shoulders before addressing me. "No growling for me, James? Not scared I'll steal your girl?"

I hear April's breath catch, her eyes glued on me. She may not be sure of my feelings on this thing between us, but I'm sure enough for the both of us.

Besides... "She already knew you and didn't ask you out, and vice versa, so out of all these fuckers, you're the safest bet."

That earns me an indignant chorus of "hey!" from the rest of the group. Cohen's eyes shine with approval and April ducks her head, a wry smile curving her lips and a gratifying pink tinge on her cheeks.

Fuck. I'm starting to sound like a girl.

"Maybe 'cause you're acting like one," Ezra murmurs from beside me.

My head snaps his way. "What?"

"You forget I know you sometimes better than you know yourself." He claps me on the back. "You're right, you are, but you deserve a woman who treats you well, who kisses you without giving a shit, and who holds on tight in the face of his boys who she knows has his back and will have hers if this goes the distance."

"Who are you and where is my best friend?"

"Ha fucking ha."

I shoot him a smirk.

"Hey, lovely. Does the swear jar apply at the driving range?" I call out, April's heat soon cloaking my side as she returns her arm around my back.

"Yep. If my little terror is going to college, he's gonna need all the help he can get."

"How much is it again?" Ezra asks her, pulling out his wallet.

"I'm sure it's two dollars a curse word," I say as April snorts.

"Fuck!" he mutters.

"Might as well give me ten and put yourself in credit, Ez. Sounds like you're gonna need it," Jamie adds.

He hands out a ten-dollar bill to April, who grabs it and shoves it in the back pocket of her skin-tight jeans that have been giving me ideas since she turned up on my doorstep in them.

"Are we playing or what?" Cohen says, holding out a driver for April.

"What's the bet, first?" I ask, Ez, April and I moving towards my brothers.

"Well, the way Jamie swears, he's gonna need all the money he can get. So how about this. The loser has to buy dinner after every golf night until auction day?" Bryant suggests, earning a round of nods from the group.

"April, since you're the new girl, you're up first," Jax says.

I chuckle under my breath as she walks to Cohen and takes the club from him.

"Do we get to choose the color of our own balls?" she asks. That has Jax, Bryant, and Cohen's eyes bugging out as Ezra and I burst out laughing.

"Let me guess; you're picking blue," I say with a knowing grin.

"Oh, you do know me well," she says with a wink. She bends at the waist, places the ball on the tee then straightens and adjusts her grip and stance until she's ready to go. "I had to do it. You know how much I like blue balls."

And when she swings and whacks the ball farther than I've ever seen a woman hit before, the only sound in the group is her satisfied giggle, proving one thing for sure.

April Williams is one of a fucking kind.

Chapter
Fifteen

April

O N THE WAY HOME FROM the driving range, I'm buzzing from not only coming third out of all of the guys but from how easy it was to join their little tradition. There was none of the awkwardness or even a warming-up period. Straight away, it was like I was one of them. Jamie also didn't act any differently, and his little growls were a mix of both amusing and arousing.

"I had a lot of fun," I announce, reaching over and lacing my fingers with his.

"I could tell." His voice is so warm I want to bathe in it—definitely a contrast from his big, gruff intensity that keeps me guessing.

"Was I gloating? I have been known to be a bit competitive."

"It wasn't your competitiveness that I was noticing," he says, low and a little raspy, a tone that also sounds very good on him.

I shift in my seat to watch him as he drives. "And what exactly *were* you noticing?"

What is it about this man that has me ready to jump him every single second I'm within launching distance? It's not just the fact I haven't been touched by a man in near-on six years; it's *him*. I've been on dates. I even had a few lackluster attempts at a kiss goodnight afterward, but no one has set me on fire from a simple look, or smartass remark rolling off his tongue.

Jamie's lips curve up, his thumb brushing over my knuckles in that way I like. "You know damn well what was distracting me," he says with a deep chuckle. "The bending, the shaking, the hair flipping. Then there was the touching and the wandering hands..."

I pull my arm free and hold my hands up in surrender. "Hey. A girl's gotta do what a girl's gotta do. I only grabbed Jaxon's ass that one time."

His eyes damn near bug out of his head. "What?" he splutters as he turns the truck into a road that snakes around the lakefront. Finding a parking spot, he pulls to a stop and shuts the engine off. Then he moves, unhooking my seatbelt and hauling me over until I'm in his lap. He reaches down and pulls the lever to lower his seat back.

"Now," he says, rubbing his hands over my shoulders and down my arms in a very measured, and controlled way that has me squirming, "let's go back to you grabbing an ass that wasn't mine..."

He dips his head and brings his lips to the bare skin of my neck, then drags the top of his tongue slowly up to my jaw then to the corner of my mouth.

"I mean, it was a nice ass. Good *genes* must run in your family. I've only felt two out of the four brothers though, so to be absolutely sure I'd have to—"

He swallows the rest of my words, his tongue spearing between my lips, his hand fisting my ponytail, holding me in place as he kisses the ever-loving shit out of me. All I can do is hold on for dear life and take what he's giving me, my moans vibrating between us. My body shifts to autopilot, my legs dropping to either side of him, my hips grinding down on his.

"Fuck you can kiss," he rasps.

"You've said that before," I pant, heaving in air.

"At least I've learned a new way to deal with your sass."

My brows lift up, a startled laugh escaping. "Is that right?"

He leans in for another kiss, this one soft and slow and light, his mouth curved into a smile. "Yep. Only a little more enjoyable than our usual back and forth."

I jerk my head, my eyes widening. "Only a little?"

His grin widens. "Well, once we get to the stage of even more physical ways to shut you up, I'm guessing I'll like those a fuck of a lot more."

I look out the window, biting my lip to hide my smile. "Another dollar," I murmur. "Best idea ever telling Ax to give you the swear jar."

"I knew it," he rasps, his hands running over my shoulders in a soothing rhythm.

Filled with an overwhelming need to be closer, I lean in and rest my head on his shoulders. His arms wrap around me.

"I thought we'd take that walk we talked about," he says quietly.

I burrow in, smoothing my hand over his chest. "I'm happy to stay right where I am."

His arms flex, and I guess I've surprised him. "Then we'll stay here."

We sit there, me making myself at home in his lap with absolutely no desire to move.

"This feels good," he murmurs as if thinking out loud.

I let that wash over me because he's not wrong, it does feel good, but more importantly, it feels right.

"I was with my ex-husband for three years from start to finish." I don't lift my head, but I do hold my breath as I wait for any kind of reaction from Jamie. I don't expect his cheek resting against my hair or his palm running up and down my back in slow, soothing sweeps.

"It was good—well, I thought it was—in the beginning. We met when I was twenty-two, and he was twenty-five. I was fresh out of college, and he was working as a salesman, selling automotive parts. It involved some travel in the beginning, but when we got married, bought the house and got pregnant, he started going away more and for longer."

A contented sigh escapes my lips. Jamie's touch is the perfect balm to help me get through this story. "Betty and I had always been close but when I had to go on bedrest for the last few weeks of the pregnancy, and with Patrick not around, she was my rock. She was even there when Ax was born, stepping in for her son who got stuck in Iowa—or so we thought. He came home a week later acting like nothing had changed and that he hadn't just missed the birth of his son."

Jamie's hand stills on my back, his legs tensing beneath me. His heartbeat under my hand speeds up, and it hits me that he's getting mad, not at me but *for* me.

I rub my cheek against his shoulder and tilt my chin up to kiss his jaw before settling back in the crook of his neck. "It's okay. I had Bets, and I had Ax."

"He doesn't sound like much of a man. Definitely not one who deserves a family like yours."

I snort at the irony of that statement because I haven't even told him the worst part. "Maybe hold that thought until I get to the end of the story."

His fingers flex against my skin as he takes a big, slow breath and lets it out, his body relaxing beneath me again. "Go on, lovely. I've got you."

Yeah, you do. The only thing that would make me feel any more comfortable would be if we were lying down, our legs tangled together.

"He never really bonded with Ax. I know some men struggle with babies because they're so dependent on their mothers in those first six weeks, but I soon realized Patrick had checked out before Ax was born. Even when I tried to get him involved, he wasn't interested." I take a deep breath before finishing. "In the end, it came out that he had been cheating on me with an eighteen-year-old receptionist in Des Moines for nine months and had also been hiding a gambling problem. So not only did I kick out a husband, Betty cut her only son out of her life, and had to move in with me to help keep a roof over our heads."

Jamie tightens his arms around me, one hand coming to the side of my face and tilting it up as he kisses me. He rests his lips against mine and seems to breathe me in. "You're fucking amazing, and thank you for sharing that with me."

All of the tension leeches from me at his words, my body melting against his.

He pulls back just enough for me to focus on him. "And my assertion stands. He definitely didn't deserve you—probably never did." *He's not wrong there.* "I hate that you and Betty had to go through that. But since it means circumstances led to you being here in my arms, it means I'm the lucky son of a bitch in this scenario."

"I dunno," I say quietly. "I'm feeling pretty damn lucky right about now."

I wrap my fingers around his shoulders and lift myself up. His head drops back. I hover over him, my body plastered to his from chest to hips. My hands slide up to cup both sides of his face.

"Just so you know," I say, lowering my forehead to his. "You're not the only one. Who would've thought I'd end up in a truck, steaming up the windows with my ignorant drunk neighbor?"

He chuckles against my lips, and it's one of the best feelings in the world.

"So, about that walk?" I ask with a smirk.

"Fuck the walk. I'm happy where I am."

"Okay," I say, settling back down against his chest, the two of us lying there in comfortable silence.

Until my phone rings from the passenger side of the truck.

I sit up and—with Jamie's help—shuffle off his lap, reaching for my purse. Pulling out my mobile, I see Home flashing on the screen.

"Hello?" I say, taking the call and letting Jamie tug me back into his side.

"Mommy?" a very sleepy Axel replies.

"Hey, baby. What's wrong?"

"I had a dream and woke up."

"What did you dream about?" I say, a huge yawn catching me by surprise.

"I was building LEGO, then the LEGO turned into a big house, so I had some pizza then kept working, and I made you a giant bedroom with a *huge* tub for you to have baths in, and then I lost you 'cause the room was *so* big."

"Oh," I say, biting my lip. "It must've been big then."

"Yeah. So, I woke up and you weren't home yet, so Gran said I can stay in your bed until you get home, but she didn't say I had to *sleep* so I…"

"Axel," I say softly. "Does Gran know you're calling me?"

There's a rustling down the phone, and my shoulders shake as Jamie quietly laughs behind me, his tender lips kissing the back of my neck.

"Noooo…" my son whispers. I can't stop myself from grinning now, my most common reaction to Axel's antics.

"Are you hiding under the covers?" I ask.

"Maybe…"

"Are you gonna go to sleep anytime soon?"

"Probably not," he sighs.

"Should Mommy cuddle you when I get home then?"

"I think so. That might help me sleep."

"Would closing your eyes and actually *trying* to sleep help you sleep?" I ask. Jamie is laughing harder now.

"Probably. But I'd rather wait for you. Then you can tell me all about your play date with Jamie."

I giggle this time, Axel's untainted innocence is so damn cute it almost makes up for the times he has me wanting to tear my hair out. *Almost.*

"How about I tell you about my play date tomorrow morning?" I ask.

Axel gasps in my ear. "Oh no, is it a sleepover play date? Kids at school have those, and they say they get to stay up late and eat junk food. You can't do that without me, Mommy. That sounds like so much fun."

That's when Jamie absolutely loses it, and I struggle to not giggle my ass off. I sit up and turn around to see him covering his mouth, his eyes dancing as he shakes his head, having obviously heard what Axel said.

"Ooh, I know. He can come have a sleepover here, and then I can have junk food too," Ax continues.

"If there's any sleepover with you," Jamie murmurs, his mouth right by my ear, "it's not junk food I'll be eating."

Holy fuck!

I struggle to regulate my breathing after that, almost dropping the phone from my hand and definitely liking Jamie's type of sleepover.

"Mommy? Are you there?"

Needing distance from Jamie to clear my head, I slide over to the passenger side. "Yeah, baby. How about you snuggle down on my bed and I'll be home soon?"

"How long is soon? 'Cause that could mean five minutes in kid time or hours in Mommy time."

This kid! "How about thirty minutes?"

"Is that half an hour?"

"It is, clever boy. Now I'm going to go now so that Jamie can drop me home and I can come steal cuddles from you. Is that okay?"

"Okay, Mommy. Love you forever."

"You're killing me, kid."

"I know," he says, like it's no big deal. "Bye, Mommy."

"Bye, Ax. Love you to the moon and back," I say, ending the call and snapping my head toward Jamie. My narrowed gaze is met with his sexy-as-fuck smirk.

"You stay over there!" I warn, pointing my finger his way. He slowly moves toward me until my hand is flat against his chest, right over his racing heart. "What will you do if I ignore you?"

My gaze drops to his mouth, and knowing just how good it feels—and how good he is at using it—makes me regret *not* being able to have any kind of sleepover with him tonight.

His eyes soften when I meet them again, and I know he understands. Reaching out, he places his hand behind my neck and gently pulls me forward, planting a soft, open-mouthed kiss on my lips. He touches the tip of his tongue to mine before pulling away and holding his forehead to mine. "Let's get you home to your boy."

"You're a good man, Jamie Cook," I say, feeling happier and lighter than I have in a long time.

"You don't know how much I was looking forward to staying up late and having junk food with you."

"Liar," I say with a startled laugh.

"Yep. But we would've stayed up late, and it would've been a *lot* of fun."

"Rain check?" I ask, earning a knowing smirk from the man beside me.

"You can bet your ass I'll be cashing that one in."

"Not if I cash it in first," I mutter, and we both laugh.

Chapter Sixteen

April

April: So that rain check we took last night...

Jamie: You mean when your son cock-blocked me?

April: In his defense, it's not like he's ever had experience with his mom dating anybody.

Jamie: So, I need to give him the birds and the bees and "Mommy has needs too" talk?

Damn, that's sweet and hot and hilarious all at once.

April: His mom does have needs, but that's nothing I can't deal with by myself in the shower.

I'm totally going to hell for that text. I imagine him reading the message, almost wishing I had X-ray vision so I could see his reaction.

I don't have to wait that long, my phone vibrating in my hand with a video call from the man himself.

"Hi." I giggle. His eyes are narrowed but scorching hot. His forehead bunches as if he's in physical pain.

"Do you know what that image does to me?" he rumbles. "Worse still, knowing that your bedroom is on the other side of the wall where I sleep and wondering whether it would be too much to knock my own hole through just so I can sneak into your room at night undetected?"

My eyes grow wide, and I reach out to grab hold of the bedpost, locking my knees, so I don't melt to the floor.

"My lovely likes that," he says, his lips curving up in the most lascivious and sexy grin. God, I love his name for me. It's meaningful and unique and just between us.

"I do. It gives me ideas that might have me taking a shower sooner rather than later."

He groans, closing his eyes and biting his lip. "Fuck... I'm hard as hell right now, and I've got contractors measuring the kitchen so I can't do anything about it."

Dropping down onto the bed, I stretch out on my back, holding the phone above my head.

"That's not helping," he grinds out, his eyes hooded and locked on mine through the screen.

"I needed to get more comfortable. The thought of you being so turned on and so close yet unable to *relieve* yourself is kind of thrilling."

"You're welcome to get more comfortable over here in about an hour," he says as a shudder travels through me.

"An hour, you say..." I switch the phone to one hand and reach down to run the tip of my finger across my lips. "I'm not sure I can wait. Do you mind if I..." I run my hand down to the neckline of my white tank, toying with the straps. Making sure to angle the camera lower, I dip inside the cup of my bra and close my eyes when my thumb brushes over my right nipple.

"Thirty minutes," he rasps, the low notes in his voice scoring a direct hit between my legs.

I open my eyes and meet his, trying to look innocent. "But your contractors..."

"Can start early on Monday. I've got someone far more fucking important to do."

I kiss Axel on the cheek, give Betty the excuse of needing to help Jamie with something—not exactly untrue, albeit slightly misleading—and walk over to the house without a minute to spare. As soon as my feet hit the top of the stairs, the front door swings open, Jamie appears, and his arm snakes around my waist. He hauls me inside. My arms loop over his shoulders just before I crush my mouth to his, his tongue delving between my parted lips, as he carries me down the hallway.

When we reach his room, his hands go to my ass. He lifts me as I jump up and wrap my calves around the back of his legs. Not tearing ourselves apart, we fall down onto the mattress, Jamie's body breaking my fall. Then I dive into action, putting my arms on either side of his head and holding myself above him as he drags his lips against my skin, trailing them over my jaw and down to my neck. A deep, desperate moan escapes me, and I swear I feel his dick pulse when I do. I roll my hips against him, wanting to drive him just as crazy as his touch is making me.

"Jamie..." I whisper harshly, my breaths coming hard and fast after he runs his tongue down my throat before sinking his teeth into the sensitive skin of my shoulder.

"Clothes. Off. Now," he spits out from beneath me, cupping my shoulders and pushing me up to straddle him. He lifts his torso so he's sitting, his legs hanging off the side of the bed. Then his hands are on my legs and moving my knees to either side of his hips.

From there, it's a blur of flying fabric and wriggling limbs as we remove my offending items at warp speed. When I go to drag my bra straps down my arms, Jamie's large, rough hands cover mine, and in a startling yet touching change of pace, he slowly inches his hands down and off, one by one. His fingers caress my face as he holds me still and moves in, brushing his lips against mine once, twice, three times before finally deepening the kiss.

When he finally lets me up for air, I sit there staring at him, my eyes glazed, my breathing labored, my heart galloping as I lose myself in the swirling depths of his hooded stare.

"Hi," I whisper, his answering smile and confused expression causing me to giggle. "Don't get me wrong; I'm not complaining about the way you greeted me at the door, but I do think it's funny that it took us ten minutes at least to say one word to each other."

"There were more important things to take care of," he says as his attention drifts over my face and down to my bare breasts now pressed against him.

I quirk a brow as I follow his gaze down and realize—somewhat belatedly—he must've answered the door in his boxers and a tee.

"Someone was feeling confident," I muse, my lips twitching. He doesn't blush or seem apologetic at all. If anything, his grin widens. "There was no time to waste. Who knows when someone could interrupt us?"

"Oh, really?" I run my hands over his arms, then bring them to rest on his shoulders. "We shouldn't delay the inevitable…"

"But—"

I catch him by surprise, shoving him onto his back and covering his mouth with mine. Then I'm sliding my near naked body against his, kissing and nipping his skin as I go. Licking my lips, I glance up at him, reveling in his blown pupils and parted lips. Jamie was rough and sexy just being Jamie, but half-naked and longing, looking at me like I am the goddess about to fulfill his every desire? He's absolutely stunning.

I run the tips of my fingers up his chest, raking my nails over his nipples then glide them back to dip under the waistband of his boxer briefs. With his eyes locked with mine, he quirks a brow as I snake my hand down and in to palm his cock. I have my skin on his, touching his most intimate body part for the first time. The heat is singeing; my entire body comes alive as if I've been electrified. Uncontrollable need surges through me, and I lose focus on my plan to go slow. I wanted to take my time, explore his body and let him discover mine. I wanted to build this from soft and tender to wild and out of control. But I should've known. We're finally alone together with all the time in the world—a few glorious uninterrupted hours anyway. I've got my mouth and hands on him, and any plans I made have gone out the window. I want it all, and I want it already.

"You stare at my dick any longer, lovely, and I'm gonna get a complex."

My narrowed gaze snaps up to his amused one, the corner of his lips turned up in challenge.

Not looking away, I lower my head and plant a line of open-mouthed wet kisses along the length of his cock through the fabric, starting at the base and ever-so-slowly working my way to the top.

"Jesus," he groans

"Jesus won't help you right now. Only I can do that."

Tapping his hips, he lifts up, and I tug his boxers down, revealing an angry, throbbing cock begging for my attention, and who am I to deny it—and me—the pleasure? I dip my head and circle my tongue around the head of his cock, then drive back down to take him all in my first go. The guttural groan I get in reply is so deep and long; I'm near on saturated and halfway to the first orgasm not by my own hand in six years.

His hand drifts down to lightly rest on my head. There's no pressure or guidance; it's more an anchor between the two of us.

I take him to the base and swallow, a ripple running through his torso as he shakes, chest heaving. He sucks in a deep breath. His fingertips biting into my scalp have my own climax threatening to make an early arrival, and there's no way I'm letting that happen without his mouth on me or his cock in me.

"Fuck, that feels so damn good." His voice is so low and deep. It's like a smooth whiskey burning its way down my throat, leaving a wave of warmth in its wake. He's so gone, and so am I. It turns me on so much more knowing I did that to him, and that he let me in to get him there.

He bends at the waist, both hands moving to my hips as he maneuvers me up and around until I'm on my hands and knees over him, my thighs framing his shoulders.

When his hand runs up the inside of my leg, and a finger traces my sex, dragging wetness as it goes, I lose any semblance of control. My eyes—and mouth—on the prize, I dip down and continue my assault.

Warm breath fans over my slick heat before his lips envelop my clit and his tongue works unheard of magic on me, my mind and body completely separating.

"Oh fuck yes," I say. I buck my hips, his nails biting into my ass urging me on as he licks and sucks and pushes one long, thick finger inside of me.

My entire body ignites, every inch of my being vibrating with need and want, wanting less and more and not knowing if I will survive the orgasm I know he's going to give me. I up my efforts, taking him longer and deeper, lifting to the tip and sucking hard before taking him to the back of my throat. He hums against my swollen nub, and I feel myself beginning to crash headfirst over the edge. If I don't survive the fall, at least I'll know I went out with a bang. I gently grate my teeth against his shaft, and he stiffens from head to toe, his tongue pushed far inside me, his finger pressing hard against my clit and circling it before rubbing it side to side.

I'm gone just as he drops his head back, grabs hold of my thigh, and digs his teeth in, grunting out his climax as Jamie releases down my throat, crying out with my mouth full as I push hard against him and slowly come back down to earth.

He runs his tongue over the bite. I know he's left a mark, and I can't wait to see it and remember exactly how it got there.

"I got a bit carried away," he rasps, his hands running down my thighs and back up my legs to rest on my hips. "Get back up here, lovely. I want to taste you again before I sink deep inside and look into your eyes while I'm doing it."

A shiver of anticipation moves through me as I shakily turn and brace myself over him. He runs his hands around my waist and up my back before pressing down, holding my body to his. Sliding his fingers into my hair, he cups my head and pulls me down for a slow, gentle, and absolutely perfect kiss. It's soft lips and languid strokes of his tongue against mine.

I lift my head and rest my cheek against his. Our lips are just touching. My heart is pounding. My girl parts continue to pulse feverishly. Jamie's chest rumbles, and he chuckles when I bury my forehead into his neck.

"You hanging in there?" he asks, playfully.

"I'm angry, and I'm wrung out, and I don't want to argue with you."

His body goes still beneath me. "What on earth do you have to be angry about?"

"Because I was supposed to make you lose control first," I huff, pressing my lips to his neck.

He shuffles on the mattress until we're lying side to side, facing each other, one of his arms under my head, the other resting on my hip.

"You're angry because I made you come first?" His eyes are wide as they take me in. "You damn near destroyed my stamina the minute you wrapped your mouth around my dick. I was ready to blow in thirty seconds flat, something I haven't done since I was fifteen and fumbling in my parents' back shed. You..." He slides his palm up my side, grazing my breast with his thumb on the way. "You taste like heaven, you suck like a dream, and in ten minutes time, I'm going to bury myself so deep inside you I won't ever want to come out again."

I open my mouth to argue—about what, I don't know—but he silences me with a hand to my jaw, commanding my full attention.

He cups my jaw, commanding my full attention. "Don't ever doubt the effect you have on me, lovely, because the first time I saw you, I wanted you, and every day since then that has only grown stronger."

"Well... dammit. I can't argue with any of that," I mutter, unable to stop myself. In one swift movement, I'm rolled on my back, my hands are on his shoulders, and he braces over me, his eyes boring into mine.

"I promise we can argue tomorrow." He dips his lips to brush over mine. "But tonight is for us, and you can be damn well sure we're going to make it count."

He presses his hips forward, his hard length gliding between my legs and making me whimper. My fingers bite into his skin as I lean up to kiss the underside of his jaw, the rough stubble my undoing.

"So, about those ten minutes..." I stare into his eyes, my heart clenching at how lucky I am to have this man in my life. It may have only been a short time, but does it matter when you're living life and enjoying the hell out of it with a beautiful man by your side?

Chapter Seventeen

Jamie

"IT'S OKAY. WE DON'T HAVE to do anything else. I just thought…" She diverts her eyes as if to look anywhere else but at me. I pinch her chin lightly between my thumb and index finger, gently turning her head to meet my stare.

"Oh, lovely, I'm fighting everything I have in me not to pin you down right now and drill you into this mattress."

Her lips part, her tongue darting out to wet them. Her eyes are blown, her gaze so scorching I can feel it like flames licking my skin.

"I wanted to make our first time together special." I cup her jaw, brushing my thumb over her skin. "You deserve special."

She looks up from beneath me, her teeth sinking into her lip, her eyes softening for the barest of instances until she snorts. Her arms move around my shoulders and drag my body down onto hers. She buries her face in my neck just as she bursts out laughing. Her chest shakes with it, her hips jerking against mine making a harder situation all that more difficult because she's naked, I'm naked, and all I want to do right now is turn that laughter into moaning.

A groan rumbles in my chest as she circles her hips in exactly the right way to have me reconsidering my plan to draw this out.

"Jamie, I love that you want that for us, but if you don't stop teasing me, I'll get dressed, go home, and get myself off in my bed while you listen through the wall, just so you know how seriously turned on I am right now."

"You think I wouldn't break down your door?" I thrust my hips against hers, loving the hitch in her breath as I run my length over her clit. I drop onto my forearms, pressing her down with my chest and running my hand down her side. I brush my thumb over her pert nipple and lower, reaching between us to trace her seam and finding her wet and waiting.

I lift up, dropping my eyes to watch my finger slowly disappear inside of her. Her body undulates as I push it deep. She clenches around me, so tight and hot. Needing more room to move, I shift to my side next to her, snaking my arm beneath her head and drawing her close so I can kiss her while I bring her to the edge again.

"I guess…" she pants as I add another finger, "you're shutting up."

"You won't be though. You're gonna scream and give me one more; then I'll give you what we both want." I withdraw and slowly push in another finger swallowing her moans as I stretch her. I run my lips along her jaw till my mouth is at her ear. "I'll show you just how special I can make you feel."

With the curve of my fingers inside of her, I find her G-spot and lift up in time to meet her eyes and watch her fall, her body tightening around me as she cries out her orgasm, her hips grinding against my hand.

I kiss her softly, easing her back down to earth. I slowly withdraw, resting my hand on her hip and deepening the kiss, loving the way she clings to me as if she's trying to get closer.

With one last stroke of my tongue, I pull back, proud of the dazed expression shining back at me.

"You still want more?" I ask hoarsely.

She rests a hand over my heart, running her fingers back and forth through the light smattering of hair on my chest. "I'm ready to show you the kind of special I want."

I dip my head and give her one last hard and fast kiss before pushing myself up and off the bed. I reach into my bag on the floor for a condom. I glance up to find April perched on an arm, watching me, her eyes fixed on my crotch, her hand slowly toying with herself as I rip open the foil packet and cover my cock.

I stalk toward her, putting a knee to the mattress and rolling her onto her back. Stroking my hand up and down my hard-on, my eyes are glued to her fingers rubbing and rolling against her skin before she eases a finger inside herself. My control snaps, and in the blink of an eye, my face is buried between her legs, wrapping my lips around her clit, and flicking my tongue back and forth to ramp her up again. When her hands move to my head, and her nails bite into my scalp, I push off and rise to brace myself above her. I lift her leg as I go and wrap it around my hips until I'm pressing the head of my cock at her entrance. Dipping down, I brush my lips against her mouth and pull back just enough to watch her eyes before slowly pushing inside her until I'm buried deep and her lids flutter closed with a soft whimper.

"You feel so damn good," I groan, easing back before finding a steady rhythm. Her hips buck against mine. She hooks her other leg behind my back, opening herself up to me as the sex goes from hot to messy in the best possible way. Her hands grip my shoulders, our lips fused together as we pant against each other, my body like a tightening spring preparing to explode. She turns her head and bites my earlobe, and it's then I know this needs to end for her before I end it far too soon myself.

I drop to a forearm and drive deeper into her, gliding my hand between us and rubbing her clit with the pad of my thumb. Three more thrusts and her entire body clenches around me, my ears ringing as she cries out her climax just as I plant myself to the hilt and growl out her name, all rational thought leaving my brain.

Rolling onto my back, I pull her over with me as we both fight to catch our breath. She rests her head on my shoulder, her warm breath coming in waves across my skin.

I lay there with April in my arms with crystal clear clarity as to just how far I've come in a short time, and how important everything I'm doing right now is to my future. I want the girl, I want her family, and I want to be the best man I can be for them, but I also want it for me. If I didn't know it before, I know I'll bleed myself dry to get there. I had a goal; now it's my mission. I'm going to make April Williams fall in love with me, and I'm going to prove that I can provide a life for us.

And I can't wait to get there.

Chapter Eighteen

Jamie

FOUR WEEKS TO GO BEFORE our ninety-day flip deadline. We're meeting at the house for our progress meeting because there isn't time to spare. We're still in catch-up mode from those lost days for the basement repairs.

Ezra walks into the now open-plan living area with a bag of food hanging from his fingers, Jase bringing up the rear with three take-out coffee cups.

"If you two were my type, I could totally kiss you right now," I announce, reaching for the drink as soon as Jase is close enough.

Jase laughs. "Well, there was this one time, at—"

"Please don't finish that sentence," Ez says with a groan. "It may well ruin my opinion of you, and I'd like to keep this professional relationship going."

Jase and I just look at each other and burst out laughing. Ezra soon joins in.

"Right," he says, after handing out breakfast burritos. "Now that you've got food and caffeine let's get down to it since we're closely approaching the business end of this little—"

I snort, which earns me a smirk.

"Okay, not-so-little project." Ezra looks around the room. "It's looking good with the drywall up now. The kitchen though…"

"That's one of the big delays. The carpenters couldn't come in last week as scheduled. It had to be put off till this coming Monday," I explain.

"That sucks," Jase says. "But I don't think we're *that* far behind, all things considered."

"Tell that to my blood pressure," I mutter, taking a swig of coffee. "I had to rebook the tilers as well, which pushed back completion of the bathrooms, which has had an effect on when the guys and I can get stuck into the painting."

Ezra sighs, turning to me. "I know you want to do as much as you could yourself to reduce spending, but I don't want you working yourself into the ground."

"We don't really have the wiggle room left to *not* do as much work as we can ourselves now, and the twins are coming over next weekend to start the front yard too."

"So, it's full-steam ahead then?" he asks.

"Pretty much. I can sleep when I'm dead," I add with a grin which is the opposite to how my stress levels are inside.

"And as far as construction is concerned?" Ezra asks, switching to Jase.

"We'll be back on schedule this week. Jamie just needs to approve the guys working OT on Saturday," Jase adds.

If I'd thought the coffee and food were helping my tension, that announcement just negated them.

I reach my hand up and wrap it around the back of my neck, rubbing back and forth as if it's going to magically make time—and money—appear out of nowhere. "Is it stuff I can do, or…?"

Jase shakes his head, and I can see the regret in his eyes. "We'll do as much as we can as quick as we can, but things like replacing the rotten framing in the garage and then knocking out the back deck next weekend, need more hands than just yours. Matt and I have already agreed we'll do any finishing touches you want on our own time, but I can't squeeze the guys much further without OT."

This is one of the reasons I work with friends. I trust them implicitly.

"Okay. But you can use me as one of the guys if you need me to. If you think it's something I can do, then I'm your man," I say.

He nods, but I don't miss Ezra's pinched features as he watches our conversation. He did warn me before I bought the house that it could consume me if I let it. He also promised he'd call me out if he saw that happening.

"Do we need to take a look around then? It sounds like you're on top of everything, but I'd hate to let my trusty clipboard go to waste," Ezra says, thankfully changing the subject.

"You and your paperwork," Jase mutters.

Both Ezra and I snort. "You're the king of fucking paperwork," I add.

"Ooh, add two dollars to the swear jar," Ezra says with a big grin. I roll my eyes and look at the ground, a chuckle rumbling in my chest.

"Not you too." I shake my head and look at Axel's—well, my—swear jar, sitting on the window frame, now at least half full with dollar bills since it's become a "site rule."

Ez holds his hands up. "Hey. Who am I to deny the kid his college fund? It's pretty damn smart to switch it from his mother to you."

"He knew he'd get more bang for his buck this way," Jase says. "Besides, maybe he's getting in early. Imagine how much he'll rake in when you become his new dad."

I choke on my coffee, thankfully swallowing down my mouthful before I'm forced to lean onto the edge of the makeshift kitchen table. I cough and splutter as I try to recover. I glare up at my two friends who are both laughing their asses off. Ezra pulls out his wallet and puts money in Jase's palm. "Knew I should've bet against him."

That gets my attention. "What?"

"Jase bet he could freak you out about dating a single mom."

"I'm not freaking out," I protest. Both men's brows lift in unison. "I'm not. You just caught me by surprise."

"Uh-huh," Ez mutters.

"April could have ten kids, and it wouldn't faze me."

Jase's eyes widen, and he clamps his mouth shut, his lips twitching as he remains fixated on the far side of the big room.

My head snaps to see a giggling April leaning a hip against the doorway.

"Ten kids? Really?" She pushes off the wood frame and crosses the room to stand at my side. "I'd say I want five more just to freak you out, but I kind of like it when you're *not* annoyed at me."

I send a half-hearted scowl down at her as she fits herself to my side, grinning up at me. "But you like it when I rile you up?" she says.

Gagging noises break the mood. Ezra holds his hand over his mouth as he fakes throwing up. "God that was awful, Jamie. April, I think you're with the wrong single man in the room. A woman should have options," he says, waggling his brows at her.

I growl and narrow my eyes at him, tightening my arm around April's waist at the same time. "Ez, if you like certain body parts where they are, you'll stop macking on my girlfriend."

April goes still, and the room goes deathly quiet. I jerk my eyes back to hers. "I mean, you are my girlfriend, right?"

When she just stares at me with her mouth agape, I power on. "Adults don't do the whole 'wanna go steady' thing." I drop my voice low when I say it.

I can tell she's trying hard to make me work for it. Her face is impassive until I spot her lips twitching just as her shoulders shake. She buries her laughter in my chest, and the guys soon join her.

I look up at the ceiling, rolling my eyes. "God, it's like I'm surrounded by children."

"Are there ten of them?" Jase asks, serving to set them all off again.

"Hey," Ezra says. "I'll be godfather to a couple, but I draw my limit at eight."

"I think my wallet will draw the limit at ten," I reply, not even realizing what I've said until the female giggle goes quiet.

"And that might be our cue to go," Ez murmurs. He shoots me a "you got this" look. I nod, and within moments, Jase is waving goodbye as he shuts the front door behind them.

I turn April to face me, running my fingers over her head, threading them through her hair. "It's just us now."

She tilts her head and meets my eyes, the soft wonder I find in them almost enough to take my breath away. "This is going to last longer than just the house flip, isn't it?"

"I damn well hope so."

"I'm a lot to take on," she says quietly.

"You're a handful alright. Axel and Betty are bonuses. They're the easy part of the package deal."

Her eyes fill with tears, her hands quickly lifting to wipe them away.

"You like that I think that, don't you?"

"No," she says. "I *love* it. And brace yourself, Jamie, because if ten kids didn't freak you out, then this probably will." She swallows and runs her hands up my body to cup my jaw. "I'm falling in love with you, and that should scare me, but I feel so safe with you. It's like letting myself go and knowing you'll catch me."

"Fuck," I spit out, tightening my grip on her hair, tilting her head and slamming my mouth down on hers. This is a woman who not only gets me, but she *gets* me. She has seen me drunk and idiotic, grumpy and surly, she can give as good as she gets, and she hasn't—not once—let me get away with anything. She works hard to provide for her family, yet she lets her guard down for me and trusts I've got her back. I was with my ex for three years, and she didn't have as much faith in me as April does, and fuck, that feels so damn good.

When we finally come up for air, her face is so bright it damn near blinds me.

"You know you owe Axel another dollar now, right?" April says with a sexy smirk.

"Fuck it." I reluctantly step back, shove my hand in my pocket, and pull out my wallet. Grabbing a one-hundred-dollar bill, I drop it onto the table, stalk over to the swear jar, and stuff the money inside. I spin around and lock eyes on my prey, her eyes widening as I stride back to her.

Before she can move, I bend down and throw her over my shoulder. She slaps my ass and shrieks as I stalk down the hallway.

"You paid too much," she breathes as I walk through my bedroom door and slam it shut behind me with my foot. I ease her to the ground, sliding her down my body so she can feel every achingly hard inch of me. Then I wrap my arms around her hips and drag my hands down to her ass. Dipping my head, I run my lips along her jaw to her ear.

"For the record, I'm already gone for you," I say, and I work my way down to her neck. "And the money was to put us in credit because after I take you to my bed, you'll be in so much debt, you'll be thanking me."

Before she can argue, I drop down onto the mattress and get my money's worth, one "oh my fucking God" and "holy shit" at a time.

Chapter Nineteen

April

SATURDAY MORNING AND I'M LYING on my back, still wrapped in a sheet. Jamie's idea of a morning wake-up call is my favorite way to spend my day off. I'd sent him a text two hours earlier when Betty had taken Axel for his swimming lesson, telling me to sleep in. Of course, with my hot boyfriend next door and the house to myself, the last thing I wanted to do was sleep. I didn't go six years without sex to find a man like Jamie and *not* have my way with him—or more like let him have his delicious way with me—at every chance available.

I lie there in my post-sex haze. His naked body cloaks my side, his hands lazily gliding over my back.

"I've gotta go soon," he says softly, not sounding like he wants to go at all. "Jax and Bry are helping me with the front yard. We've got to remove the old pavers, dig a new path, and frame it up for the cement to be poured first thing Monday."

"I can help," I offer on the back of a huge yawn.

He chuckles, pressing his lips to the back of my neck and sending a ripple of goosebumps across my skin.

"Axel might want to join you. He never likes missing a chance to work," I murmur, my lids closing as he teases me with feather-light kisses and barely-there brushes.

"He's more than welcome. I might even buy him a little shovel to dig with."

"He'd love that. Every time he helps you, you'd think you were the stars, and you'd hung the moon."

"He's a good kid. An extortionist in training, but he's definitely a character."

My mind goes blank. Those two orgasms must have numbed my brain cells. "You're good at this dad thing," I blurt out.

His hand freezes in the small of my back before he must catch himself and try to hide it. *Too late for that.* That's enough to snap me out of my post-climatic haze.

I lift up on my elbows and scramble to sit, bringing the sheet with me, feeling suddenly and overwhelmingly exposed. My eyes meet his guarded ones. I open my mouth to backpedal, to say something—anything—to take the words back, but I don't get the chance, because Jamie is reaching out and brushing his thumb over the apple of my cheek.

"I didn't mean that," I say.

"You don't think I'll be a good father one day?" he asks, his brows bunched together.

"I've only known you for nine weeks."

"And would you normally let anyone meet your son after nine weeks?"

"If a man had impressed me enough to get past the first date and was still around and full of promise after nine weeks, then sure," I say with a shrug.

Then, in a move quicker than the Flash, I'm flat on my back, and Jamie is lying on top of me. His forearms frame my head, his face filling my vision. "So, I ticked all your boxes after that first date?"

"Well, you were planning future dates before we even started our first date."

"Oh, we'd started. We started the minute you barged into the house and rescued me."

I roll my eyes but can't stop myself from watching his gorgeous face transform, his knowing grin and amused gaze confirming what I already knew. He had my agitation and attention the moment I first scolded him. But I've never—not once—wanted any man I got involved with to think I was searching for a new baby daddy. Axel has done fine without a father for the past six years, and he could do fine without one for another six. My interest in Jamie has purely been for me, and only me. The fact that he has won over Ax has served to endear him to me even more.

"Whatever happens between us is separate to what I've got with Ax," He says, his gaze firm, his body unyielding as it holds me in place.

"Yeah, I know... I didn't..." I stutter.

"We're both old enough and experienced enough to know you don't get involved with someone in the way we're involved with each other without wanting it to go somewhere. Me asking you out had nothing to do with me wanting just what we have in this bed. It was about wanting everything you were willing to give me. Axel is a bonus, and if you already think I'll make a good father one day, then I can't wait to see me rocking it when I get more experience."

Damn it. "That's a really fucking good answer," I whisper, my voice cracking as my eyes fill with tears. His gaze softens before falling to my mouth, then intensifies in the split second before he drops his lips to mine. His tongue spears inside. He swallows my guttural moan as he rests his full weight against me, making me feel anchored and safe, and so damn hot.

That's all we say for the next twenty minutes because the second I hook my arms around his back and my ankles behind his hips, Jamie loses his self-control and starts riling me in a completely enjoyable way. If I thought I was having trouble thinking straight before, afterward, when Jamie rolls out of my bed, gets dressed, then brushes his lips against my temple with a murmured, "See you later, lovely," I barely have the energy to lift my head, let alone talk.

"By the way," he says, stopping in the doorway, "send Ax over after he's had lunch, and tell him if he's late, I'll dock his pay."

I rally enough to lift a brow. "You don't pay him."

Then he winks at me. "Yeah, but he doesn't know that."

Best. Morning. Ever.

"You called me over, telling me I *had* to come visit, and now we're just sitting on your front porch? What gives, April?"

"Just wait..." I murmur, lifting my wine glass to my lips. Ronnie is beside me, Betty beside her. My best friend arrived five minutes ago, and the second she stepped inside, I was ushering her back outside to take a seat and prepare for the show.

"Wait for what? You're acting very strange," Ronnie says with a frown.

"You won't be complaining soon enough," Betty murmurs, her eyes glued to the yard next door.

"So, how's Jamie?" Ronnie asks me, still not sounding convinced that Betty and I are of right mind.

I turn my head to face her. "He's awesome," I reply, a wry smile on my lips, the same lips still tingling from just a few hours earlier when Jamie paid them—and the rest of my body—a whole lot of much-appreciated attention.

Her soft gasp fills the air, her eyes pinned on something behind me. I slowly spin back around to see Jamie walk out from the side of the house, a faded Cubs baseball cap turned backward on his head, a white wife-beater clinging to his chest, his shorts hugging his muscular thighs, and planks of timber slung over his shoulder. He's soon followed by a shirtless Jax carrying the other end of the wood in a similar fashion, Bryant and Axel coming behind them with shovels in their hands.

"Mmhmm," I hum, instinctively licking my lips at the sight before us. My eyes are glued to Jamie who glances over toward us, a knowing smirk twisting his lips.

"Ladies," he calls out, his smile widening. I lift my hand to wave just as Axel sees us and returns the gesture with enthusiastic muster.

"Aunt Ronnie!" he cries out, jumping up and down excitedly before looking up at Bryant, tugging his tee. "That's my Aunt Ronnie. She's awesome. She buys me LEGO."

Bryant shoots my son a grin before looking over at the three of us ladies at the same time as Jamie and Jax lower the timber to the ground. Jax lifts his arm and swipes it over his forehead, the breathless sigh escaping Ronnie's lips making me giggle.

"Twins," she says approvingly. She turns back to look at me. "I'm guessing Jamie is the bigger one?"

My eyes widen. "What makes you say that?"

"If looks could undress, you'd be naked as the day you were born already."

"They definitely aren't hard to look at," Betty adds, making us all laugh.

I take another sip of my wine, no longer able to tear myself away from the guys and Ax as they each take a shovel and drive it into the ground, muscles flexing and tightening in magnificent ways.

"This seems so sexist, but I really can't seem to make myself care," Ronnie whispers.

"Fair's fair. Think of all the construction sites women walk past and get heckled and ogled from," I reply.

"Oh, I don't know," Betty says. "Enjoyable shows of masculinity like this are meant to be savored. We'd be doing womankind a disservice if we stopped watching now, especially out of some misplaced belief that we don't have every right to do so."

I laugh and spin in my seat, holding my glass in the air for both of them. "Hear, hear. Besides," I say, raking my eyes over Jamie as he shifts dirt from the new path to the garden lining the front of his porch, "I'm simply supervising my son."

That starts us all laughing, earning amused looks from the Cook boys. Axel frowns and waggles his finger at me. My son can tell me off as much as he wants, because until my man is covered up and no longer tempting me with all those sweaty muscles, that tight ass of his, and those bulging arms and broad shoulders, I feel it's my duty to watch him do what he loves.

That's the excuse I'm going with anyway.

A few hours later, I can see Ax fading but not wanting to show it around the guys. I crack open three cold beers from the fridge and a soda for Axel. With Ronnie in tow, I walk along the sidewalk and down Jamie's driveway to rescue my boy.

After handing the soda to Axel and ruffling his hair with my hand, I move toward my other man.

"Hey," I say, walking right up to Jamie, beer in hand. He leans his shovel against the porch railing, holding out a hand for the beer and then lifting his arm up for me to fit underneath, tucking me into his side when I'm close enough. He brushes his lips against my hair. "Enjoy the show?" he asks, dropping his mouth to my ear.

"If you're lucky, I'll show you just how much later tonight."

"I should work in my yard more often," he says with a husky chuckle.

"My yard is your yard. Do whatever you like with it."

He nips my ear, dropping his voice to a whisper. "Change that to 'do whatever I like with you,' and we've got a deal."

"And now I wanna be sick," Jax announces, earning a round of laughs. Even Axel joins in, no doubt not knowing why but doing it anyway.

"Behave," I warn, playfully smacking Jamie's chest.

"With you around, I'm not making any promises," he says confidently.

I see Ronnie has handed the other beers to the twins, her hands empty when I catch her grinning at me before switching her attention to Jamie with her arm outstretched. "You must be Jamie—otherwise my best friend has been checking out strangers again. Not that I'm condemning her for it."

Jax bursts out laughing, Bryant's lips turn up, and Axel's little head moves between all of us as he comes up to my side.

Jamie shakes her hand. "And you're Ronnie? April said you were coming over today."

"She didn't mention you guys would be hard at work. I almost feel guilty for having to sit over there with a glass of wine and just watch."

"Oh, don't feel guilty," Jax says.

Ronnie giggles. "Oh, I didn't; I said *almost*. We were simply supervising Axel. Right, Ax?"

"That's what responsible adults do," Jax replies, his body turned toward my best friend's. *This is an interesting development.*

"Exactly. I'm just fulfilling my duty as his aunt and godmother." Ronnie's lips curve into a smirk.

"Aunt, 'ey? So, you and April are sisters?" Bryant asks, before taking another swig of his beer.

Ronnie and I look at each other and snicker. "Not by blood, but we may as well be," she answers.

"Nice," Bryant says, nodding in approval, but his body language is in complete contrast to Jax's. He is watching Ronnie closely, his eyes shamelessly raking over her just as hers had obsessed over him when we'd been watching them from the porch.

"April tells me you're flipping this place, Jamie. How much more to go?" she asks.

He nods, following her eyes to look at the now sanded-back exterior of the house. The roof was finished this week. I know there's still a lot of painting and finishing to be done, but construction inside is finished. "Three weeks until we're supposed to be putting it on the market. It'll be a tight squeeze to get it done in time, but working day and night, I'll get it done."

"And he'll tell his brothers when he needs help, won't he?" Bryant adds, staring his older brother down. I thought Cohen was the intense one, but right now, Bryant is giving him a run for his money.

"Wow. So, what happens when you sell it? Is this a one-time thing or something you do?" Ronnie says.

"This is our first one. Jamie is working it full-time while us two and our younger brother, Cohen, still hold down our day jobs and help out whenever we can."

"So, you guys want the glory, and Jamie is the muscle?" Ronnie asks.

"And the brains," Jamie says wryly, not appearing to be bothered by Ronnie's inquisition. "But to answer your question, provided we make a profit on this one, then it's full steam ahead onto the next one."

Jax nods. "The plan is we'll each be able to take a leave of absence from our jobs when we start to see a real turn-around. Then, who knows? We might all be working this gig."

"Let's get this first one under our belts first," Jamie teases, but I don't miss the tic in his jaw and the tensing of his body. Definitely something to bring up with him later.

"It's gonna be finished in time, Jamie. You've got enough people willing to step up and help," Bryant adds.

"Yep. I'll help you, Jamie," Axel says, beaming up at my man.

"See? With Axel on the job, we'll definitely finish. Look how much we got done today with his help," Bryant adds. These Cook men sure know how to make a little boy's day.

Jax grins before upending his bottle, finishing his beer, and holding his bottle in his hand. "That went down well."

"Damn, straight," Bryant replies, holding up his hand for a fist bump with first Jax, then Axel.

"Yeah," Ax says. "Damn straight."

"Hey, Ax, you want a beer?" Ronnie asks teasingly.

"Yeah," he replies, his eyes wide.

"Too bad," Ronnie says, making us all laugh. Jamie makes me melt when he reaches out and rubs Axel's hair the same way I do.

"We've got more drinks at home, guys. I was gonna invite Ronnie to stay for dinner, and Jamie was coming over anyway. You guys are welcome to join us," I say, looking between Jax and Bryant.

They swap looks and both nod. "That sounds great. Thanks."

"And then I can show you my LEGO, Jax," Ax says, craning his neck up.

Jax grins down at him. "Yeah, Axel. Can't wait."

The beaming smile on my son's face has me blinking to stop from tearing up. Ronnie shoots a pornographic look Jaxon's way. When he catches her eye, there's no mistaking the reflecting interest either. This could get messy, but I've never been one to stop her when it comes to following her heart—or her other body parts. Ronnie is Ronnie; she was repressed for so long by family pressure and the weight of their expectations. She's been slowly coming back into herself and seeing a flash of the wild child best friend I thought I'd lost. I'm not gonna stop her from doing anything—or anyone—she wants to. My job is to be there in the aftermath, whether it be good, bad, or ugly.

"Well, we'll go back home and start getting the food ready. You guys come over whenever you're done," I say to the group.

"Sounds good, lovely," Jamie says, tilting my chin up with the top of his thumb and planting a hard, fast, and lust-inducing kiss on my lips.

"Oh God, Ronnie, take her away before we see more than any of us want to see," Jax groans.

"C'mon, Ax. We need your help picking the food for dinner," my best friend says.

"Oh yay," he says, his little eyes looking relieved. He looks up to Jamie. "Is it okay if I go home now, Jamie? Have I done enough work?"

"Buddy, you were so much help today. Thank you." Jamie holds his hand out for Axel to shake, making any chest swell with pride. My words from this morning echo in my head. *You're good at this dad thing.*

Every time I see Jamie and Ax together, Jamie proves my sentiment true.

This may be a new relationship, but the way I feel for Jamie, the way he feels for me, and the way he is with Axel prove one thing. Moving from slow and steady to fast and full-on isn't always a bad thing, especially when it feels so goddamn right.

It feels like everything in our lives has been leading us to this—and each other.

Chapter Twenty

Jamie

Monday

April: Hey. Are you still coming over for dinner tonight? I can bring you a doggy bag if you're still busy?

Jamie: Shit. I totally lost track of time. I'm knee-deep in paint right now and don't have time to stop. Are you working tomorrow? I can't remember what you told me.

April: Yeah, I start four days of twelve-hour shifts from tomorrow night.

Jamie: Lunch tomorrow then? I'll bring the food; you bring your smile.

April: Okay. Make sure you sleep tonight. I could always come help.

Jamie: It's going to be a late one. I'm looking forward to seeing you tomorrow. I miss your lips.

April: Sweet talking will almost make up for missing dinner.

Jamie: Guess I better keep it up then.

April: You've never had a problem in that department.

Tuesday

April: How's your night going? I'm on a dinner break so thought I'd check in with you.

Wednesday

Jamie: Sorry I missed your message last night. I was doing the finishing touches to the master bath. I'll try and catch you before your shift tonight.

Thursday

April: Jamie, I'm getting worried about you. I know you're under the pump, but you've gotta take care of yourself. Come sleep here once you've finished for the night. At least then I can make sure you're fed and getting some rest.

Jamie: Only if you're sure. I don't want to keep you up.

April: Worrying about you IS keeping me up. Just let me help in any way I can.

Jamie: You're too good to me.

April: I know. I'll expect payback at some stage.

Saturday

April: I woke up and you were gone. You were supposed to kiss me goodbye first. I'm going with Betty and Axel to swimming this morning, but Axel and I can pop around this afternoon to help you with anything. Just let me know.

Monday

April: Missed seeing you yesterday. I hope you're doing okay. Not too long to go until you'll be finished. We should celebrate when you do. Let me know where.

Jamie: I'm the one who's supposed to be paying you back, remember? I'll make a reservation and let you know.

Tuesday

April: I can come over tonight and help you. Just let me know, and I'm there.

Jamie: After working all day, I can't ask you to do that. You take it easy. I'll call you tomorrow.

Coming into this project, I knew a ninety-day flip would be a hard ask. It wasn't just the fact that we were doing it on a tight budget, or that out of us four brothers, I was the only one doing this full-time. This project is my baby; the one I quit my job for and went all in on.

When Jase, Ezra, and I sat down after I first found this house, we came up with a plan that—although ambitious—was achievable. That was after Jase, Ez, and I did a walk-through and noted what needed to be done in every room, to every part of the exterior, and in the garage. It didn't include some "wish list" things that I'd hoped to get time to do—mainly replacing the fencing—but it also didn't anticipate having to repair April's garden, spending an extra eight thousand on fixing a cracked basement wall, or losing four days off the schedule when the site was shut down because of it.

That's led to now, another night I should be spending with April and Ax. Instead, I'm here at the house. I've got old walls to be resurfaced, new walls to be smoothed out and primed, old *and* new walls to be painted along with the doors, bathroom vanities and cabinets to be installed, tiling to be done in the laundry, and then planting in the front and back gardens. Next, I have to stage the house with Mom and Abi before meeting with the agent, all in a week and a half.

Try as I might, I've let the pressure get to me, and as much as I didn't want to let it affect my personal life, thanks to the lack of time and not wanting to let anyone down—my brothers, Jase, Ezra, myself—I'm epically failing. I've called off the driving range tonight, and I'm covered head to toe in dust. Despite working all day with barely a break, I'm hungry and tired, yet determined to keep going.

I rationalize that this is only for two more weeks, then I can sleep, and spend time with April and Ax, and maybe even go out somewhere with just the three of us.

I need to get the house finished, staged, on the market, and hopefully sold quickly—then I can breathe a little more freely. I have to make this work. I'm more determined than ever to turn this venture into a successful business, one that can be profitable for both me and my family. Also, one that can help me build a future and prove to April that I can—and will—support her and Axel. That I can be the man for them and be an equal partner as we work toward our future.

My phone rings from the kitchen where I purposefully left it so I wouldn't be distracted. Now more than ever, I can't afford to make any mistakes. Knowing I should answer it, I lower my face mask, shake myself off, and move down the hallway, catching Cohen's name flashing on the screen before the ringing stops. I press redial and call him back, hearing him answer the phone without it even ringing.

"Hey, still alive there?" he asks. "I saw April at the hospital today, and she mentioned you might be feeling the pressure."

That answers that question. I'm obviously already failing at hiding my stress from April. Enough for her to say something to Cohen anyway.

"I'm okay. Just busy," I reply.

"Yeah, and you're also you're own worst enemy when it comes to keeping things to yourself and not letting people help you."

"I don't need help."

"Says the man with twenty thousand dollars of his brothers' money invested in this."

"Thanks," I snap back. "Good to be reminded that I couldn't do any of this without the help of my *younger* brothers."

"Age has nothing to do with it, Jamie. It's your inability to *let* us help you—willingly, I might add—without thinking it's detrimental to you in some way. We didn't go into this with you because we didn't think you could do it without us. We did it because we know you can, and we want to be part of your dream."

Fuck, that feels good. He doesn't give me much of a break before he keeps going.

"And I know you've been working every waking moment—and probably some sleeping ones—getting the house finished, but you've gotta cut yourself some slack."

"I don't have slack to cut, and I'm the one who quit everything to do this flip. You guys all have full-time jobs."

"We all knew that going into this, and we know this is your baby, but we're willing to help you get to the finish line. The delays weren't your fault; neither was having to spend the spare money on the extra roof repairs, the basement, and even April's fence. There are so many people waiting to help you, Jamie."

"I don't think I've heard you call me Jamie this much in years. I must really be in trouble."

"Don't worry. You'll always be James to me."

"Good to know. And Co?"

"Yeah?"

"Thank you. I know I haven't been good to be around."

"It probably isn't me you need to explain any of this to. Get to the end of this, take her out, talk to her, and let her in."

"I have…"

"I mean share, unload, tell her why you work as hard as you do. Let her know everything you want and why you're running yourself into the ground to get there."

"It's for them."

"Yes, but it's also for you to provide a future. April is one of the smartest women I know. She's probably worked it all out already, but you need to make sure she knows that it's for the future you want with her and Ax—not just for you. United front, and all that."

"When did my twenty-nine-year-old brother get to be so smart?"

"It's from watching you fuckers screw up your lives."

"Thanks for the pep talk, Co. I may not be the easiest person to be around sometimes, but—"

"You should know, out of everyone, you're my emergency contact. You're the person who I'd call before anyone else in the family. If I am in trouble, it's you. If I need a smack around the head, it's you. If I need an organ—"

"I get it," I say with a smile. "Thanks, Co. I think I needed you to tell it to me straight."

"Is it gonna change anything?"

"Probably not for this project, but I will talk to April. I'm not willing to lose her for anything—not even this house."

"That's the thing you haven't realized yet. You're not going to lose her, but you may lose yourself if you keep trying to make everyone happy. You're no good to anyone if you're dead on your feet and unable to function outside of working on the house."

"Has April said something else you're not telling me?"

"You have a mighty fine woman there, Jamie. Get the house done, then work your ass off to make it up to her. That's all I'm going to say."

I hear the bells down the phone, signaling he has a callout.

"Look, I've gotta go. But keep me updated on the house, and if we have to, we'll turn the driving range night into a 'save Jamie's sanity' night instead."

"There you go with the *Jamie* again."

"Bye James," he says, ending the call, leaving me with a grin on my face.

Now I'm torn.

The house has to come first. I'll apologize and grovel to April as soon as it's all done and I have time to make it up to her and Axel.

A week and a half—that's all there is to go, then we've just gotta hope it sells quickly, all while finding the next house to flip.

Should be easy. Maybe…

With one day to spare and with my brothers, Ezra, Matt, and Jase at my side, I screw in the final light bulb in the ornate yet apparently inexpensive light fitting in the center of the living room. A roar of applause breaks out.

I feel the weight of the world ease off my shoulders, knowing that step one of the plan is now completed. The house has been finished before the end of business on day ninety. Well, six p.m. on day eighty-nine is almost as close as I could get to deadline, but fuck does it feel good.

April sent me a text earlier telling me she was working an extra hour to cover for a friend and suggested we change our reservation for another night. As much as I wanted her to be here, I have my own plans for the two of us. Starting with dinner for two at the same Mexican restaurant we had our first date at. I felt it was fitting that we go back to where we started so that I could show her how I plan on continuing.

I've made a point to keep in constant contact with her. I've tried to hide the strain of the looming deadline from her, not wanting to put any burden on her shoulders that is all mine.

I've snuck over and stayed the night a few times in the past eight days, especially since Cohen figuratively punched me in the face with the truth. I'm not an island, and I shouldn't act like one—not when I have a woman like April and the promise of a future with her.

Half a glass of champagne later, I kick everyone out, promising to update them all as soon as the agent takes possession and we confirm her marketing plan for the house. A quick shower and outfit change later, and I'm standing on April's front porch.

"Hi," I say, the moment she opens the door.

"Hey." She looks amazing, but she sounds tired—maybe a little flat. "You look stunning."

She's wearing a white sundress which has short puffy sleeves and a fitted top that falls to just above her knee. It's sexy but still demure. It's totally April.

"You look tired," she probes.

"So do you, but you still look a darn sight better than me." I step forward and wrap my arm around her waist, brushing my mouth against hers. When I step away, I catch a small smile gracing her lips. *That's a start.* "Besides, nothing could keep me away from you tonight."

"You're finished then? The house is done?" She sounds almost hopeful. I've really made a bit of a mess of this. I can only wish that she gives me a chance to explain and make it up to everyone.

"Yeah. I just have to meet with the real estate agent tomorrow to hand the keys over, get Jax to take the photos for marketing, and confirm the open home dates."

"And you're sure you're up to this tonight?" We're still standing in the doorway. Normally, I would've been invited in by now. I would've said hello to Betty and talked with Axel for a while before we said good night to him and left to go out. Nothing about this seems normal, and it's only been three days since I was last here.

"April, what's wrong?"

Her eyes are wary—or maybe more. She shakes her head as if to clear it, calls goodbye over her shoulder, and steps out to join me on the porch, shutting the door behind her.

I reach out to lace my fingers with hers, and thankfully, she lets me. That's one concession at least, but it doesn't mean that I'm feeling at ease about our dinner and what may happen. The April I help step up into my truck is not the woman I've fallen for. I miss the sass, I miss the spunk, and I'm willing to do anything to get it back. I'm not clueless, but I've definitely been an idiot.

That's all about to change though. Whatever I have to do, whatever it takes, I'm going to earn back the sass, the spunk, the smart mouth, and the fiery side of April—everything about her that I've fallen in love within three months. I never thought it would happen like this. I didn't see it happening for a few more years in fact, but once I saw her, there was never going to be anyone else.

By the end of the night, I'm going to make sure she knows deep in her bones that there will never be anyone else for her either.

Chapter Twenty-One

April

FOR TWO WEEKS, I WAS patient. I tried to play the patient, caring, understanding partner. Then I started to get angry, and—surprisingly—these past few days, I've been waiting for Jamie to just disappear from my life completely.

I'm an open-minded woman. I know how important finishing the house renovations before deadline was to Jamie, and I'd never ask him to choose me over his business. But some consideration would've been nice. Axel has even noticed Jamie's absence and has been asking questions I don't have answers to.

"When will Jamie help me grill hot dogs again?"

"Will he still be my boss when he builds another house?"

"Will Jamie move away when he's finished?"

I even spoke with Cohen at the hospital last week, and he assured me that Jamie was naturally an over-worker—something I had noticed myself—but that he also lets his protective provider streak take the wheel sometimes. Now *that* is news to me. Doesn't mean I'm going to let him get away with shutting me out for the past few weeks. Cohen told me that I need to talk to Jamie and let him know how I've been feeling. Bottling up anything will do nobody any good.

A few days later, Jamie called me to say he wanted to take me to dinner tonight and that he'd made reservations at the same restaurant we went to on our first date.

I tried to postpone, my nerves getting the best of me today, but the fear that tonight may be the end of our relationship won out. That was hours ago. Now, sitting in a leather booth near the back of the restaurant, the server sliding new drinks onto the table and clearing our plates, I know I can't put off this talk any longer. It's not fear that's holding me back though; it's frustration.

Over dinner, we exchanged small talk. He excitedly told me about completing the house and how good it feels to be finished, and then he went through what has to happen next. I've participated and responded when necessary, but my patience at him not bringing up his lack of communication while he finished the house has now run out.

I lift my margarita to my lips, closing my eyes and taking a long sip, letting the liquor give me the boost I need to confront Jamie and effectively, lay all my cards out on the table. When I meet his wary gaze again, I know it's now or never.

"April?" he says, reaching across the table for my hand. When I move it away, his brows bunch together.

"If you touch me, I'll lose my nerve."

His body tenses, his eyes snapping to mine. Not once have I ever shied away from him. Until now. "Tell me what's wrong so I can make it right."

I lift my drink to my mouth again and down it, putting my glass back on the table and resting my arms in my lap. If this is ever to work between us, I'm going to have to put myself out there.

"Please talk to me, lovely." The sound of his name for me from his lips washes over me, and although he doesn't realize it, that's the last push I need.

I move around the booth so I'm sitting beside him, I *need* to be close to him. Sitting across the table from each other is putting distance between us, which—having had enough distance from him in the past few weeks—I don't want anymore.

"Something you might have realized about me is that I'm a nurturer. I want to help people. I want those I care about to be the best they can possibly be, and if I can help them get there, then I'll do anything I can to support them," I say.

When he reaches for my hand, this time, I don't stop him. In fact, I meet him halfway. His shoulders sag, and a sigh escapes his lips

"It has been six years since I have taken a chance on a man, and then I—"

He opens his mouth but I shake my head once. His almost imperceptible nod tells me to continue.

"Then I met you, and you sparked something in me. You challenged me. You didn't sweet talk me or even try and chat me up. You took my sass and kept coming back. I almost believe you got off on our arguing at the start."

"I still do," he murmurs, and for the first time tonight, I feel hope. Maybe he does just need to know how shutting me out has made me feel.

"Then you wore me down with your flirting and garden replacing, and when I saw just how good you are with Axel—with no ulterior motive behind it at all—I made the choice to see where this might lead."

"You sure it wasn't me cornering you against the side of your house and *persuading* you to go out with me?"

My lips quirk up on one side. "Maybe," I concede. It's the only concession he's going to get from me though. "I fell for you, and every single day that passes that I spend with you, I fall deeper. This isn't temporary for me. I have never introduced any man to my son, and I always said that I never would until I knew that it was going somewhere. It was a way to protect Ax but also, myself."

He brushes his thumb over the back of my hand, encouraging me to go on.

"You're the first man in my life that Axel has met, and I almost think he was falling for you right alongside me."

"That feeling is mutual, April. You've gotta know just how much you mean to me."

I close my eyes and let his words wash over me before I reopen them, clear my throat, and let my last wall down, crossing my fingers that I'm not wrong about this. "These past three months, you let me see your soft spot—the one you hide behind that cocky smile and smart-ass bravado—and when you did, I was hooked in such a way that I knew I'd never want to be unhooked ever again." His entire body goes still, but I power on, knowing I have to or else I'll never say what both of us need me to. "But for the last few weeks, you've hidden it from me. You've been acting like you think you're alone in this. I've already told you I've been with a man who hid things from me, who didn't tell me about the ups and downs—"

His eyes flash. "I'm not—"

I squeeze his fingers in mine. "No," I say, leaving no room for doubt. "You're *nothing* like him, but you pulled away from me—from us—and became so tunnel-visioned and focused on the house that every day you've lost track of time, or have been too busy or too tired to even see us, or you've slid into my bed at midnight only to be gone again by six. It's put distance between us."

"I never meant it to."

"The thing is, Jamie, it's been giving me flashes of a life I don't want, and it has scared me. It's had me doubting what we have for the first time since the moment we got together, and I hate feeling like this." I see the moment the truth in my words hits home. It's like a light bulb goes off, his eyes wide and his lips parting, and his hold on my hand tightening.

His head drops down as he slowly closes his eyes and brushes his hair back off his face. When he lifts his gaze to mine again, I swallow a gasp at the change. Almost instantly, he's let the shutters open.

After lowering his mouth to my hand, he presses his lips to my knuckles, his kiss so soft and reverent I have to blink rapidly to stop the tears falling. This is Jamie—*my* Jamie—coming back to me as though he'd never left. Thought I'd never admit it to his face, Cohen was right to encourage me to put it all out there. Jamie just needed a figurative slap around so he knew what he'd been doing.

"I never want you to ever feel that you're second place in my life. You and Axel mean the world to me, just as much as my family. The house is just a house, but I know that I lost myself somewhere in the past few weeks. It kills me to think you started to doubt me—*us*—because of my dumbass behavior."

Just like that, the tension I'd been holding in my shoulders leaches out of my body. "I know you've been under pressure, and that's why I haven't said anything until now. But you have to understand that although I'm always going to be on your side, there's more than just the two of us in this relationship. I can cope with a lot more than you think, but I don't like being shut out and you not letting me help when that's all I want to do."

"I know. And I've been an idiot." He looks down at our entwined fingers, and I swear I see him blush.

"Can I record this?" I ask, pretending to reach for my phone. He gently squeezes my fingers, and for the first time in ten minutes, I see his lips twitch before his eyes roam over my face.

"My ex of three years broke up with me because she didn't think I could make something of the business and wasn't prepared to wait around to see what happened. Then my brothers insisted I let them join me, and that felt better than anything. They believed in me and trusted me to make it work. The thing is, at first, I was doing this for myself, to prove to anyone who ever doubted me that I could make a living out of doing what I always wanted to. But that's now changed..."

"It has?" I ask, my eyes transfixed to his.

"Yeah," he says. "Because now I'm doing this for me, but I'm also doing it for you, and Axel, and our future ten kids."

I let the tears fall. How could I have doubted I was in love with this man? "And I would never not support you in doing what you've gotta do and working toward your dream. Just like I know you'd always support me in following my own destiny. I want to build a future with you, one that includes you being present and involved. I want you to be free to give us every part of you during the good, the bad, *and* the hard times. Dreams should be shared with the people in your life who mean the most to you, but you've also got to be willing for them to help you get there. I want to know I did everything I could to help you get to where you want to be just like I know you'll always do the same for me."

He sits there staring at me like I've just dropped a reality he never even contemplated. "I want you to be a part of my dream, April because you and Axel are the missing piece of my puzzle. I just thought..." He looks down at our joined hands. I let him go and lift my arm to cup his jaw, waiting for his eyes to meet mine.

"You just thought what?" I whisper.

"I thought I had to reach my goal before I could let myself have everything I've ever truly wanted."

"And what was that?" I ask.

There is no mistaking the intensity in his stare and the absolute certainty in his tone when he rocks my world with one single word.

"You."

Chapter Twenty-Two

Jamie

I DON'T THINK I'VE EVER paid a bill and left a restaurant any quicker than I did tonight.

I don't want to be in a room full of strangers. I want to be in a room alone with April, with nothing between us, where I can dedicate the rest of the evening to worshipping her until she can take no more.

That's not the only reason we rush back to her house after only an hour. It's because I want to see Axel. I want to apologize to him and help tuck him in before he goes to sleep. We also want to let him know that I'm going to be staying overnight.

Knowing I'm the only man in April's life who has spent time with Axel makes me more determined than ever to prove to both of them— and Betty too—that I'm not going anywhere. As long as they'll have me, I'm going to be in their lives. I want a true fifty/fifty partnership with April. I want her to be able to lean on me as much as I know I can— and now know I *should*—lean on her. It's like she schooled me on how a true adult relationship should be, and I don't want to give her any reason to doubt my feelings and commitment to her ever again.

I pull the car to a stop in her driveway. April goes to hop out of the truck, but I put my hand on her thigh to stop her.

She scrunches her forehead adorably—she'd probably have my balls if I told her that—and turns to face me. "What's wrong?"

I lean forward, closing the distance between us and lifting my hand to slide my fingers through her hair and cup the back of her head. "I got one more thing I need to say before we go inside."

"Okay…"

I let my gaze roam over her face, watching her teeth sink into her bottom lip. By the time I reach her eyes, my heart is thumping against my chest. I never expected to be in this place in my life with a woman who thrills me, supports me, and never fails to challenge me. The woman who I truly believe was made for me in every single way and who thankfully just happens to live next door to the house that is the start of a dream that I know deep in my soul she represents the end of.

"Jamie?" she asks, her frown deepening.

"I was half gone the minute you walked through my door." I shake my head, my mouth curving up into a smile. "But the first time I kissed you, I knew I was done for. You're it for me, and I want to spend the rest of my life by your side, at your back, and in your bed." I swallow hard before I say the words. "I love you, lovely, and I never want to stop."

Her mouth drops open before curving up in her sexy smile. "I love you too, *James*," she says, her grin beaming at my growl. Then she can't do anything but moan once I tug her head toward mine and lay a long, wet, very deep kiss on her lips that has her melting against me.

When I let her go, I hear a giggle coming from outside the car. As if in slow motion, we both swivel our heads to the porch steps to see a waving Axel and a smirking Betty. *That's one way to let them know everything is fine I suppose.*

"Shit," I spit out, quickly looking back at April to gauge her reaction.

"Well I guess *that* makes it a little easier to explain why you'll be here in the morning," she says. My eyes bug out, but she simply swipes her thumb across my bottom lip and grins. "Wanna change your mind?"

"Fuck no."

She tilts her head and grins. "We better get in there; otherwise he'll come in here, and he's already told us how much he *loves* your truck and he can't wait till he's old and can get a 'big truck like Jamie.'"

I chuckle at that, wondering just how much of a handful Axel's gonna be when he's older. After one last look at his mom and the undeniable happiness I see on her face, I realize that I can't fucking wait.

"By the way, you owe the swear jar two dollars, and probably another five for your thoughts," she says with a smirk.

This time when she goes for the door, I don't stop her. But once I'm outside, I take her hand the second she's within reach, and we follow Axel and Betty inside.

Axel is a ball of energy as soon as we're through the door, quickly tackling his mother's legs and saying a quick hello before grabbing my hand and near-on dragging me up the stairs towards his room.

"Good night, Axel," Betty calls from the bottom of the stairs leading up to his room. "And you too, Jamie. I'm off to bed to read."

"Good night," I say before I'm pulled into Axel's room and toward his bookcase.

"Mommy said you wanted to read me a book, so I've been trying to decide which one to choose."

"And did you pick one?"

"Um, first I picked this one." He picks up a picture book with a plane on the outside. "Then I thought that was too short and you'd read it in no time," he continues, his voice full of animated excitement.

"Why don't you pick your favorite, and we'll read that tonight. Then the next time I'm here for your bedtime, I can read another one... if you want me to."

Axel's eyes widen, a huge smile appearing soon after. "That would be *awesome*," he whispers. "Okay. Then I really do like this plane one."

I nod in agreement. "Then that's the one we'll read."

"Okay," he replies, bounding over to his bed and quickly jumping under the covers. I turn my head toward the door where April now leans against the frame.

"Mommy, are you staying to hear Jamie read to me?" Axel asks.

Her features are soft as she walks over to Axel and bends over the bed to kiss his cheek, before lovingly smoothing her hand over his hair. "I think I'll sit this one out, Ax. Do you remember what I said on the phone earlier?"

He nods quickly. "Yep. You said Jamie might spend the night and have a sleepover with you." He looks past April to me, his brows furrowed. "But Mommy said there would be no junk food, Jamie. I hope you have fun though."

I try to keep a straight face, but the moment I see April's eyes shining my way, her teeth biting into her lip as she tries hard not to laugh, I lose all hope and start grinning.

"How about the next time I sleep over, we make it a late night with junk food and movies?"

Axel gasps and claps his hands. "Cool!"

"Sounds like we've got a plan," April says, turning back to the bed. "Are you okay with Jamie staying the night in Mommy's bed? You're the man of the house, so if you don't want him to, he will go home and come back in the morning."

I've never seen a kid roll their eyes in a "duh" motion until now, and going by how quickly—and how well—he does it, he's definitely perfected the art at an early age.

"Mom, I'm a big boy. I'm okay with missing out on a sleepover. Besides, Gran said sometimes adults spend the night and that Jamie is your special friend, and since he's also my friend, he's allowed to stay over. But next time," he says with a grin, "Gran said Jamie can stay in *my* room instead."

April barks out a laugh while I stand there with my mouth gaping open. I was about to make a note to buy Betty a bunch of flowers and a bottle of wine for helping pave the way for me, but after that little nugget of information, I'm suddenly rethinking it. It seems the spunk is strong in this household.

"I'll leave you guys to it." April gives Axel another kiss. "I'll see you in the morning. We can have pancakes if you want?"

"Yes!" he says with a little fist pump. "Jamie, Mommy makes the *best* pancakes in the whole entire *world*."

"Does she really?" My eyes take in April as she straightens and walks over to me. Wrapping her arms around my shoulders, she brings her lips to my ear.

"I'll be in the shower if you need me," she whispers before kissing my cheek in the exact same way she did with her son and moving out of the room.

I watch her go, loving the extra swing in her step. Not for the first time in the last three months, I wonder how the hell I got to be so lucky.

"C'mon, Jamie," Axel says, patting the side of his bed, and without any further delay, I carry the book with me and sit on the bed beside him. Together, we read a book about planes that may be too short but is a memory I won't soon forget.

Chapter Twenty-Three

Jamie

I SENSE APRIL BEFORE HER lips press against mine. Slowly opening my eyes, I find her wearing my T-shirt with a pair of black workout pants.

"Why are you dressed and not *undressed* in bed next to me?" I ask.

She snickers against my mouth before straightening, ruining my perfect view that went down the front of my too-big-for-her tee. I pout, and her eyes soften as they drop to my mouth.

"I was enjoying the view," I say.

She scrunches her forehead before her eyes widen and she gasps. "You're such a pervert."

I hold my hands up in the air. "Guilty as charged, but I'm *your* pervert."

She bites her lip, and it takes everything in me not to wrap my arms around her waist and drag her back onto the mattress. "I liked waking up with you lying next to me," she says quietly.

I roll onto my side and pull her down to sit on the bed in the crook of my hips, my hand slowly sliding up and down her back. "I'd like to say that too if you weren't a blanket hog."

Her mouth gapes open, her tiny hands flying to her hips as she moves into the petulant woman pose. "Take that back. I am *not* a blanket hog."

My lips twitch, and I can't keep up the facade. "No, but your reaction makes it totally worth it."

Her eyes narrow as she points her finger my way. "You don't deserve coffee in bed now. And here I was, trying to be nice despite all the sexing I didn't get last night."

"I'll make it up to you. I just put my head down for a second while you were locking up and the next thing I knew, it was morning."

Her expression softens. "Lucky for you, Betty is taking Axel to school, I have the day off, and *you* are going to rest for at least half the day. Girlfriend's orders."

She leans over as if to steal the steaming cup on the nightstand away from me, giggling when I move it out of her reach.

"I'm watching you, Cook," she says, her smile telling me she's full of shit.

Leaning against the headboard, I lift said coffee to my lips, closing my eyes as I savor the offering from the coffee gods. I'm so bone-tired from trying to keep up with everyone and everything. After bleeding myself dry to get the house finished on time, I've been mainlining anything caffeinated for the past few weeks. Hopefully, now that the house is done, I can reduce the caffeine and start living a bit more of a normal life… until we take possession of our next house, that is.

I shoot her a mock salute, earning me narrowed eyes before she shakes her head and walks out of the room.

Soon after, I hear footsteps running down the hallway before a disheveled and surprisingly fresh-faced Axel fills the doorway. He skids around the corner and rushes to the end of the bed before launching himself onto the mattress.

"How was the sleepover?" he asks in all his childhood innocence. I can't wait to embarrass him with these kinds of stories when he's older.

"I fell asleep as soon as my head hit the pillow. How about you, buddy?"

"Me too. I closed my eyes and counted to fifty like you said, and I fell asleep, just like that."

"That's good. I told you that trick works."

"Yeah," he says, before wringing his hands in his lap, shifting his weight from side to side.

"Jamie?"

"Yeah, buddy?"

"So, are you my new dad now?"

I open my mouth to say something, but nothing comes out.

Before I'm able to find the power of speech again, he continues, "But you're my boss too?"

I decide to play along. "Your boss?"

He nods. "At the house. Building and stuff."

"Well, not exact—"

"So that makes you my dad boss then?" He has the most serious look on his face, and I'm totally out of my depth here.

"Um…" I look to the door, willing April to walk through it and save me.

"Dad boss then," he says again with a nod. "That's good. Means I can get more money now."

I cough, reaching over to the nightstand to take a long, much-needed drink from my coffee cup. I say the only thing that comes to mind: "Sure thing, buddy."

"Awesome," he says, a huge smile transforming his face. "Then I can buy flowers for Mom, so the next time you break our garden, I can fix it and make her smile like you did."

"That's awesome. Now… have you seen my pants?"

"Are you not wearing pajamas?" Without warning, he lifts the sheet covering me from the waist down. "Oh, you've got big boy boxers like me. Mommy says I can only wear them when I wear shorts though. Are you sure you wore pants last night? Maybe you wore shorts because you've got your big boy boxers on." And thank fuck I kept them on before falling to sleep last night.

"I was definitely wearing pants. Do you want to look in the bathroom for me?"

"It's okay. I don't need to. I saw Mommy carrying them into the kitchen."

"Lovely?" I yell, hoping she can hear me. When a loud beat starts coming from downstairs, my bullshit sensor starts pinging. April is up to something, especially since it's the exact same Queen song I was playing the night we first met. *Two can play this game.*

"Should we go get pancakes?" I ask.

"Yeah!" he says, jumping up and down before running out of the room.

I move to the bathroom and use the facilities. Searching for my clothes, I come up empty. Sure enough, my pants have indeed disappeared. With nothing else left to do about it, I walk out of the bedroom and down the stairs, wearing nothing but my boxer shorts.

I stop still the moment I enter the kitchen. Just as I'd imagined, April is sitting at the dining table, coffee in hand, her legs up, her ankles crossed on a chair with a wicked smirk on her face. Her only saving grace is the huge plate of pancakes piled high in the middle of the table.

"Hey Ax, how's breakfast?" I ask.

"So good," he groans, stuffing another forkful of pancake in his mouth.

"What are you doing after school today?"

His head snaps up. "Nuff-thing," he says with a mouthful of food.

"Good. I was thinking you could bring your mom and gran over and we could give them a tour of the house now that it's finished."

"Oh wow. Yeah," he says, puffing out his little chest. "I can show them where I worked."

"Yep," I reply with a grin. With his attention back on his rapidly emptying plate, I move in front of April. "You look good in my tee. Did you also find my pants on your travels?"

Her lips twitch. "I thought I'd do some laundry."

I lean down and brush my lips against her cheek. "Just you wait, lovely," I whisper. "I'll be claiming my shirt off your back the minute Ax and Betty are out the door."

Her breath catches, and when I straighten, I see lust swirling in her eyes.

"I'll hold you to that," she replies, sounding a little breathless now.

I run my eyes greedily down her body and back up again. "Oh, there'll be holding alright."

We stare at each other, our hungry gazes so hot we'll probably start a fire if we aren't careful.

Axel groans, looking up from his plate and tilting his head as his gaze switches between us. "Adults are weird," he says with a harrumph before returning his attention to his plate.

And just like that, the spell is broken. With one last look at each other, April and I burst out laughing.

Four o'clock that afternoon, we meet the real estate agent and Jax outside the house. I'm surprisingly nervous. Not about the agent seeing the house and officially putting it up for sale, but about what April will think of it. She hasn't been inside the house for almost three weeks, something that was completely my own stupid doing. I know now more than ever that sharing this with her is important. It's letting her be a part of my dream.

"Wow," she breathes when we walk through the door. Mom and Abi worked with a friend of Cohen's to stage the place with pieces of furniture collected from my storage unit and our houses. In future, once we have a profit behind us, we'll look into using staging companies, but we decided to go this route to keep our costs down.

Axel and Betty follow in behind April, Jax and the agent going on ahead to the bedrooms. April stands in the middle of the living room, her eyes wide as she takes a slow, sweeping turn.

"Jamie, this place is…"

"*Awesome!*" Axel says, running ahead into the kitchen. "Mommy, come look at these cabinets. I helped put the knob on this door."

Betty walks past us, stopping to pat me on the back and press a kiss to my cheek. "You've worked miracles, Jamie. This place is amazing. It'll sell in no time," she says, nodding in approval.

"It better, otherwise my bank manager won't be a happy man."

"It will, Jamie," April says, moving to my side and wrapping her arms around my waist. "This puts our renovations to shame, right, Betty?"

"Well, our budget was probably a quarter of what Jamie spent on this one, but I love the feel of it. It's a real family home," Betty replies, her voice filled with pride.

Axel comes running into the room, grabbing for Betty's hand. "Gran, come look at the backyard. Me and the guys planted all the flowers. It was *so* cool."

"I can't wait. Lead the way, Ax," she replies, shooting us a wink before being dragged away.

April turns so we're chest to chest, her arms resting on my hips. "You should be so proud of what you've done here."

I look around the now huge open-plan living/dining/kitchen, realizing that I actually am proud. All the hard work, the late nights, the cuts, the scrapes, the aching muscles, and the constant reminders that I'm no longer in my twenties—they were all worth it.

"I am. This house means a lot to me. It's Cook Construction's first official project. We finished a day before deadline despite everything and the best thing of all…" I say, running my hands up her back and pressing her closer, "I got drunk and needed medical attention from my sexy, sassy, *spunky* neighbor."

Her eyes narrow on the word sassy, but shine bright on the word spunky. "You forgot highly intelligent, patient…" she says, her mouth curving up on one side.

"And she looks fucking fantastic in and out of clothes," I murmur against her lips.

"That's a dollar," Axel announces, bounding into the room. "Eww, are you guys kissing *again?*" He makes gagging noises just as Jax and the real estate agent walk back into the room. "Jax," he moans. "Jamie and Mom are kissing again. Tell them to stop."

Jax shakes his head, looking down at Axel with a knowing grin. "Just you wait until you have a girl on your arm as pretty as your mom. Then you'll want to kiss her too."

"When I'm a big boy?" Axel asks, making us all chuckle.

"Yeah, baby, when you're thirty," April says, letting me go. "Now, can you show me and Gran the rest of the house? Then Jamie and Jax can finish up their business talk."

He nods and grabs hold of each of their hands, the three of them moving toward the hallway, but not before giving Jax a high five.

"This place is stunning, Jamie. You have all done an amazing job here. I can already think of a few of my clients who are looking for a new home just like this one," Jacqui, the agent, says, walking into the kitchen. "The revised layout, the addition of the study, the new appliances and kitchen—they're all going to be huge selling points."

Jax grins at me, and I can't help but do the same.

"What are the next steps?" I ask.

"So, Jax will take some photos for me—since he's the professional photographer—and send them through. I'll give those clients of mine a call and try and schedule a few viewings, and I think if they don't pan out, then we'll definitely go ahead with open houses next week. Believe me; I don't see this listing being on the market for very long at all."

I breathe a sigh of relief. "Fingers crossed."

She reaches into her messenger bag and holds out a small stack of papers to me. "I also pulled these potential properties for you all to look at. Just let me know if you want to go see any of them."

"Will do. Jax is thinking about helping with one of our projects in the future. Right, Jax?" I say, nodding toward my brother.

"Yep."

"Oh, are you taking time off work?" Jacqui asks him.

"More like taking a step sideways. I'm going to be teaching a few college courses on photography and graphic design in Summer, so I'm hoping I can help Jamie work on a future flip project. 'Cause looking at this place, jeez, he could really use some help, right?" he says, a huge shit-eating grin on his face.

I shake my head at the smartass, wishing I could call him an asshole, but we have company, so that's out of the question. "Ha ha."

"You guys are hilarious," Jacqui says. "Well, I've got to go, but leave a key in the lockbox on the front porch, and I'll be in touch whenever I need to bring someone through," she says before turning to me. "Jamie, are you still going to be living here until the house sells?"

"I was planning to. I'm hoping it won't be long before we close on the next house, so I shouldn't need to crash on my brothers' couches too much."

Jax looks past us to the hallway where April, Betty, and Axel emerge, the three of them smiling.

"I'll go. See you all next time," Jacqui says, waving goodbye to the room and walking out the front door.

As if there's a magnet between us, April and I meet in the middle of the room. "You know you can stay with us. I know you would never ask, but you're welcome to if you find yourself between houses."

I dip my head and place a gentle kiss against her lips. "Oh, I'll be having a lot of sleepovers, but we're not ready for living together. Not right now, because when I move in it won't be temporary, and it may not even be next door."

Her eyes go wide, her breathing slightly erratic.

"Especially since your place isn't big enough for ten kids," I say.

Her giggles fill the room and Axel looks up at his mom with a frown. "Ten?" he whispers.

"Now, I don't know about you, Ax," Jax says, "but I'm craving a deep dish from Giordano's. How about you?"

The boy's eyes go wide as saucers, and I swear, he looks ready to cry with happiness. "I think you're my new best friend."

"What about Adrian?" April says, hooking her thumb in the belt loop of my jeans and holding me close. "I thought he was your 'bestest friend in the whole wide world.'"

"Hey," I say, mock glaring at Axel. "I thought *I* was your best friend. We bonded over hot dogs, LEGO, and books about planes." I add in a fake pout for good measure.

Axel moves his head between Jax and me, and back to Jax, then back to me. Then he throws his hands in the air and growls. "Ugh, I can't choose, so you'll just have to share me," he declares before storming out of the house in all his moody six-year-old glory.

"God, I love that boy," Jax says with a laugh. "He's like the coolest kid I've ever met."

I look to April, then back to my brother. "Join the club, brother. Join the club."

Chapter Twenty-Four

April

THE PAST FIVE WEEKS HAVE flown by, and Jamie has stayed true to his word to not shut me out. He's been present in every way, staying over a few nights a week and taking us out on the weekends to do family-like things. We even took Axel with us to the driving range last Saturday.

Jamie has been going out of his way to prove to Ax and me that we're now his priority. I already knew I had nothing to worry about, but when I see him interact with my son and treat him like he's his own flesh and blood every day, I fall more in love. I've never been happier.

The house next door sold a few days ago with an all-cash offer and a ten-day close. Soon we'll have a nice young couple and their eight-year-old son as new neighbors, and Jamie has already secured a new house to flip a few neighborhoods away. Proving how small the world is, the new owner, Mark, used to be in the Coast Guard with Jamie, and Mark's wife, Audrey, and I have already bonded over having sons determined to turn us prematurely gray.

Today, though, is the first time Jamie's taking us to his parents' house to experience what he calls "survival of the fittest," also known as a full family dinner with all the brothers, Ezra, Jamie's sister, Abi, her husband, Cade, and their adorable son, Harry.

I thought I'd be nervous. I've met everyone already, but somehow, this seems like the last frontier. Jamie even said if I can survive tonight, then there will be nothing I can't handle. Instead, it's Axel who is uncharacteristically quiet in the back of Jamie's truck as we find a parking spot outside Jamie's parents' house.

Axel sticks to Jamie like glue as we knock on the door and let ourselves in.

"Hello, hello," Jamie's mom, Marcy, says, rushing down the hallway to greet us. She squats down in front of Axel. "There's my favorite six-year-old. How is Nana Marcy's big boy?"

Axel beams, his body relaxing in front of my very eyes. Marcy looks back to Betty and I. "Hey, April. Hey, Betty. Mind if I steal your little man here?"

Jamie chuckles, Betty snorts, and I shake my head, smiling down at Axel. Typically, he just can't help but charm everyone he comes in contact with, especially the ladies. I hate to think what any son of Jamie's would be like. We'd probably need to start stockpiling condoms for their teenage years when they were born.

"Shoo, everyone else is in the backyard. Go relax," Marcy says, ushering us in that direction.

"I'll come help you in the kitchen," Betty says. "Let's leave the young folk to talk about whatever they talk about."

"Young folk," Marcy says with a snort. "Rick is out there with them, and the last time he was classed as 'young folk,' he was charming me out of my pants at Lollapalooza."

"So last year then?" Jamie muses.

"My boys, always disrespectful."

"Love ya, Mom," he says, taking my hand and stopping to kiss his mom's cheek before ruffling Axel's hair and leading me down the hall and out into the backyard.

As soon as we walk outside, everyone stands and applauds, including Marcy, Betty, and Axel at the back door behind us.

"What on earth?" I whisper as I spot a "congratulations" banner on the fence.

Jamie's dad, Rick, is the first to come up to us. I step away just as he holds out his hand to his son, shaking it, then pulling him in for a huge bear hug.

"Proud of you, son," he says in his ear before letting him go and wrapping his arm around my shoulders. "Now you come sit by me."

"Hey, old man," Jamie says, jokingly. "She's mine, remember?"

God, I'll never get sick of that.

Rick looks back at Jamie to shoot him a wink. "Enough with calling me old. You're only as old as the woman you're feeling. So right now, I'm feeling twenty years younger," he says, making me giggle.

Jamie shakes his head, making sure to brush his hand around my hip and over my ass as I walk past. He doesn't even need to claim me, but knowing he likes to do it, and the *ways* he likes to do it, makes me giddy every single time.

As promised, Rick guides me to a chair next to his at the table, as the twins and Jamie partake in a little roughhousing and Cohen moves towards me. "What would you like to drink?"

"A wine would be fantastic. Thank you."

"I thought I'd offer because it might be a while before the twins let Jamie go," Cohen says.

I look over to see Jax trying to put Jamie in a headlock and Bryant standing beside them, laughing his ass off.

"Jesus," I say in disbelief. "If this is what boys are like, I hope we only have girls. Ax is enough of a handful."

Abi holds her glass in the air. "Amen to *that*. Harry had me up half the night wanting to play. That kid is almost as demanding as his father."

Cade leans over the back of her chair and whispers something in her ear that makes her cheeks turn bright red. It must be something absolutely filthy to make her blush.

"She never complains when I keep her up at night," he says.

Abi rolls her eyes, but from the stories I've heard from Jamie about Cade and Abi's relationship, I don't doubt it for a second.

"Hey, April. Nice to see each other out of scrubs for once," Cade says.

"Who needs normal clothes when you work as much as we do, right?"

"Too true," he says, just as Cohen places my glass of wine on the table in front of me.

I glance over to Jamie to see Ezra has saved him from double trouble. Axel has now joined them, standing by Jamie's side, his new favorite place.

Sitting here surrounded by everyone who loves Jamie, it brings home just how much he has given us. It's always been the three of us and Ronnie since Patrick left, my parents living down in Florida and Betty's husband having passed away before I'd even met her. Axel has never been short of love, but now he has an abundance of it. We've been welcomed into this family with open arms, and I can't imagine things could get any better than right now.

I don't even realize a tear has fallen onto my cheek when Jamie and Axel corner me in. Jamie bends down and around, Axel doing the same on the other side.

"What's wrong?" Jamie asks, his brows bunched together.

"Nothing," I say with a trembling smile. "I'm just being an emotional woman."

"In a good way, or a 'you're gonna have to bail me out once I deal with the person who upset you' kind of way?"

Axel holds up his hand, flexing his fingers before tightening them into a fist. "Yeah, who do we need to beat up?"

My head jerks back and I look at him like he's grown another head. "Who are you and where has my son gone?" I ask, my lips twitching.

I look back to Jamie who is totally struggling to keep a straight face.

"Calm down, Hulk and Ant-Man. I'm fine. They're happy tears…"

"I thought I was more Thor myself. What about you, buddy?" Jamie asks.

"Definitely Iron Man. I'm not an ant."

Jamie nods approvingly. "Good call."

"*Hello?* Crying mom here."

"Mommy, you're not supposed to cry when you're happy, silly."

Jamie quirks a brow at me, his eyes roaming my face as if to make sure I'm okay before he turns to Axel and imparts some apparent male wisdom. "Buddy, girls cry when they're happy; they cry when they're sad. They also cry when they're angry."

"Chicks, man. Sheesh." Axel rolls his eyes, then runs across the lawn to where Bryant, Jax, and Ezra are playing with baby Harry.

"What made you so happy?" Jamie asks.

"You do."

"I'm glad, lovely. But you've gotta give me more than that."

"Being here with everyone. It just hit me that you've given us more than you realize, and I'm so grateful for it. I got a little overwhelmed. Us *chicks* do that sometimes," I say with a wry smile. His eyes drop to my lips.

"Even when you cry, you're goddamn beautiful," he murmurs. He leans in to kiss me, a soft, slow touch of his lips to mine.

"Get a room," one of the guys calls out.

Jamie snorts, kissing me again before lifting his head and shouting, "Get a life, Ez." I giggle, loving the constant back and forth between the guys. "I've been hearing his voice for years. I'd know his bullshit anywhere," Jamie says, his eyes crinkled.

"You owe a dollar," I say with a smirk. Axel's swear jar now lives on my kitchen counter, but out of all of us, Jamie is definitely the highest donor.

"I shoved a hundred-dollar bill in there this morning. I'm in credit." His grin is huge.

"Are you gonna keep sucking face or actually sit down and say hi to your favorite sister?" Abi asks. When Jamie takes the spare seat beside me, there's no missing Abi's approving grin. "Hey, James."

"Not you too," Jamie groans.

Abi shrugs. "Co says it's your favorite name so who am I to argue."

"Co is full of shit," I mutter."

"Yes, yes I am," Cohen says, snickering from his perch at the end of the table.

"Dinner time!" Marcy announces, Betty and Rick by her side, the three of them carrying multiple dishes. All the Cook boys jump up out of their seats to help.

"Now I know why it's called survival of the fittest," I mutter, watching with avid fascination as the bodies clamber to fill their plates first.

"Buddy, you better get over here before you miss out," Jamie calls out to Axel. He shoots me a wink, something so simple reminding me how happy I am. Then he proves he's perfect by preparing my plate as well.

After everyone has finished eating, Cade appears at my side with a squirming baby Harry in his arms. "Hey, April. Would you be able to hold this wriggle monster for me?"

I look up at him and grin, holding my hands out to grab the little menace-in-training.

"Spitfire," Cade says, beckoning Abi with a crooked finger. "I need to discuss something with you inside."

One look at Abi's face and I know *exactly* what they need to do. So does everyone else, if the rolled eyes and grimaces are anything to go by.

"Dude! That's our sister," Jamie groans.

"Yep," Cade replies, his smirk huge.

"Take all the time you like. We'll just play pass the baby while you play hide the—"

Jamie's hand covers my mouth, muffling my words while everyone within earshot laughs. Even baby Harry giggles and claps his hands.

"Aww look, Mommy. He likes you," Axel says, running to my side and laughing when Harry reaches out and grabs hold of my son's hair.

"Babies like everyone," I say with a shrug just as Harry is stolen from my lap by Cohen, and Axel moves down the table to sit in Betty's lap. Then it's just Jamie and me.

"He's got Cook blood in him. He knows a good woman when he sees one," Jamie muses.

I look his way, quirking a brow. "Like you did?"

"Abso-fucking-lutely," he says, placing his hand behind my head and gently pulling me in for a toe-curling kiss that is borderline inappropriate. His eyes bore into mine, and in that one look, I can feel just how much he loves me.

"What was that for?" I ask, my breathless voice giving away how affected I am.

"For being everything I needed when I didn't know I needed it, and for giving me shit. For being the kind of woman who'll barge into her new neighbor's house and scold him for being drunk and dumb, and for giving me one of my dreams while supporting the other."

"Damn, I love you," I mutter, my tears falling freely now.

"Love you too, lovely. Love you forever," he says, sealing it with a brush of his lips over my temple.

"Hey Jamie, are they happy tears again?" Axel asks from Betty's lap at the other end of the table.

"Yeah, buddy. It's our job to make sure they're always happy tears. You up for it?"

"Abso-fucking-lutely."

"Axel!" we say in unison.

Marcy gasps, Betty frowns, Rick grins, the boys burst out laughing, and Ezra chuckles. Great. The one time my son swears, and it's in front of everyone. *Murphy's fucking law.*

If ever there was a perfect way to sum up our journey during the past four months, my son saying his first curse word in front of Jamie's entire family would definitely be it.

And I would not change a single thing.

But with Jamie as his role model, and Jax, Bryant, Cohen, and Ezra as his cohorts and partners-in-crime, should I have expected anything less?

Epilogue

A S PER TRADITION, I'M STANDING on a step ladder, screwing in the last light bulb on our third completed house flip. Also, compulsory now is champagne for the ladies—Mom, Betty, April, and Abi—and beer for the men. Axel gets soda or juice; his choice changes with every house. For this particular project's celebration, he's chosen apple juice.

With three flips under our belts, we're now carrying a much healthier bank balance, and with each new project we embark on, we're continuing to learn new ways to do things. We've also managed to shorten the flips to close to seventy to seventy-five days with the aim of reaching a sixty-day turnaround by next year.

Not once have I let the stress and pressure I put on myself get overwhelming, and April has played a major role in that. Her support for what I do, and my desire to do it has never wavered. She has been my rock, a very welcome distraction when I need it. Even with her long shifts and my demanding project deadlines, we continue to make spending time together and spending time with Axel our priority.

My brothers have also been helping me out more. Jaxon is all set to work alongside me on our next project because that house will be a little different. It's also the reason why I'm ushering April out the door and into my truck, leaving Axel behind with Betty.

"Where are we going?" she asks, her fingers laced with mine, her mood happy and curious.

"It's a surprise."

"Do I get clues?"

"Nope."

"Is it a sex club?" she asks like that's an everyday, normal question to ask your partner. As always, she's keeping me on my toes.

"No. But I reserve the right to further investigate your interest in visiting such an establishment."

"What?" she gasps.

"You heard me." Out of the corner of my eye, I see her tilt her head as if trying to get a read on me.

I sigh. "Let's just say I know someone who knows someone."

"Well, shit. That kind of backfired on me, didn't it?" she says with a laugh.

I grin at her, dragging my eyes down her body and back up again. "*Definitely* revisiting that topic again."

"No!" she gasps.

"Totally."

"You're joking," she says, her breath catching. "You'd never let anyone else see me naked."

I grin. "They have private rooms. I know the owner."

"Jamie! No!" Now her laughing is more nervous.

I decide to put her out of her misery. "You're right. But your reaction was so worth running with it."

She lets go of my hand and whacks my arm. "You'll pay for that."

"I'm betting on it. In fact, as soon as we're done with your surprise, I'm more than willing to take my punishment, wherever and whatever you deem fit. As long as you're naked while you're dishing it out."

She growls under her breath, making me chuckle.

"You're adorable when you're trying to be feisty."

"I'm not trying. I'm plotting ways to dispose of your body."

I flick on my indicator, turn into a driveway, and pull the truck to a stop. Then I'm undoing her seatbelt and dragging her across the seat so she's sitting right next to me. Turning my body toward her, I hook my hand behind her head and tug her mouth to mine, plunging my tongue between her lips and kissing her until her body sags into mine.

"If you kill me, who else could do that to you?" I whisper in her ear before I straighten and lean back against the truck door.

She shakes her head, her eyes narrowing. My smile gets bigger the longer she tries to pretend she's annoyed.

It's then she looks out the windshield, her eyes widening as she takes it in. The house is three levels—two stories and a basement—with a big front yard, and even bigger backyard that she can only just see beside the garage in front of us. It's a renovator's dream, and this is going to be the biggest project I've ever done. But there's some more important business to attend to first.

"Wait there," I say, jumping out of the truck, rounding the hood, opening the passenger door, and holding my hand out to April. Locking the truck behind me, I lace my fingers with hers and lead her up the front steps and onto a wrap-around porch. Letting her go for just a second, I find the right key on my key ring and slide it in the lock, opening the door.

I start the tour on the lower level, pointing out features I want to keep, talking about plans Ezra and I have already started to work on together, and then telling her about all the things we're planning to do to the rooms. Then I lead her up the stairs to where the master suite will be, a room that will take up half of the top floor and include a small balcony overlooking the back of the property.

"So, what do you think?" I ask, stopping on the edge of the room.

"It's amazing. It's just the kind of house I hope to buy one day. With a lot of love, this place will be even better once you're finished with it." Her smile is radiant; her eyes drifting around the room as if she can't stop herself. "What about the other houses we looked at? You never showed me this one."

"The others were great, but this one is different," I say softly.

"It's so much more than just different."

"Yeah..."

She tilts her head to the side, her gaze turning skeptical. "What aren't you telling me?"

My lips twitch. "I can't get anything past you, can I?"

"Well, I damn well hope not," she says with a laugh.

I walk toward her, place my hands on her hips, and draw her in close. Circling her wrists in my hands, I lift them up and loop them over my shoulder before my arms snake up her back.

"It's different because I bought it for us. We can renovate it exactly how we want and then—if you're ready—all four of us can live here."

Her eyes are now glassy. Her lips part and for the first time since I met her, I think I've rendered her speechless.

"I wonder if Betty would like to live on her own again?" April says softly, her voice rough.

My heart stutters, the final part of the dream I once thought impossible now within my reach. I can feel my fingertips almost touching it. "I want to build a life with you and Axel. Betty is more than welcome. As long as it's you I come home to, you I go to bed with, and you that I wake up to, I'll be happy."

She looks around the room again, her small smile growing larger than life. Then it's as if time stops still and my chest is collapsing in on itself until she nods, small at first, then faster, and suddenly, I can breathe again.

"Yes, I want to make a home with you. A life, a future," she rushes out. "God, I love you."

She launches herself at me. My hands clamber to catch her under her ass as she wraps her legs around my hips and kisses me like her life depends on it. I deepen the connection, and I never want it to end. Reluctantly, I gently ease her back down until her feet are firmly on the floor.

"So, we're really doing this?" I ask, needing to hear it one more time.

She cups my jaw in her hand, and I lean into her touch. "Yeah, we're really doing this," she whispers.

"Then you are going to need this." I reach into my pocket and pull out the house key I had cut for her yesterday. I brush my fingers over her knuckles and lift it up between us. I open her palm and carefully place the key ring in her palm, closing her hand over it.

Leaning in, I rest my head against hers, taking a second to breathe her in and calm my nerves. I thank my lucky stars that I'm the one who gets to have April Williams by my side for the rest of my life. "Open your hand, lovely," I murmur.

Shifting back, she opens her hand, unfurls her fingers and looks down. Her entire body goes still. Her eyes are glued to her hand because on the key ring I just gave her is a house key, but there's also a beautiful solitaire diamond engagement ring. Watching her face, I see the first tear fall onto her cheek, soon followed by another and another.

Unable to resist, I hold her face in my hands and kiss her again, this time soft and slow. Our eyes are locked on one another, my heart close to bursting. When we pull apart this time, I look over her shoulder and smile.

I place my hands on her shoulders and gently spin her around toward the door to see Betty and Axel standing there, huge grins on their faces. In Axel's hand is a big bunch of his mom's favorite flowers, and Betty holds a bottle of champagne and a can of soda.

Cupping my hand on her cheek, I tilt her face toward mine, then whisper the most important question I'll ever ask, "April, will you marry me?"

With her eyes brimming with tears, she says the word that makes me the happiest man on the planet. "Yes!"

Axel cries out an enthusiastic "whoop" before running to us, tackling our legs, the flowers in his hand an unfortunate casualty as they drop to the floor. In a moment like this, I don't care. I'll go out and buy a hundred more bouquets.

When we step apart, Betty is there, holding out the champagne and glasses for me, and handing the can of soda to Axel. Then April looks over at her and loses it, pulling her mother-in-law in for a huge hug as they both cry in each other's arms.

"I'm so happy for you," Betty says, both women pulling away with a smile and tear-filled eyes.

"Not as happy as I am," I say, sidling up to them and wrapping my arm around April's waist and holding her close.

"Does this mean we're moving, Mommy?" Axel asks.

I lean down and lift him up in my arms, bringing him between us. "It means that all of us are going to work on this house and make it absolutely perfect for us."

"Really?" he asks, excitement dripping from his words.

April giggles. "Yeah, baby."

"Does this mean I get to paint my own room too?" he says, his voice getting louder and more high-pitched.

I chuckle as April grins at her son. "Yeah, buddy. I'm going to need a lot of help with this one. We've gotta make Mommy happy. You up for the job?"

He nods furiously. "Absolutely. I'm your man."

God, I love him just as much as his mom. "Then you're hired."

"Yay," he says, wriggling down to the ground and running over to the window overlooking the backyard. "Wow. It's so big!"

I turn back to Betty and April—my *fiancée,* a title that will change as quickly as possible to wife. "Should we go grab dinner? We've got reservations to celebrate."

April pops a hip and quirks her brows at me. "You were that sure I'd say yes?"

I lean in for a hard and fast kiss. "I was pretty damn hopeful."

"Lucky for me."

"Oh no," I say with a laugh. "I'm the lucky one."

"As long as you keep believing that, you're gonna do just fine, Jamie Cook," she says with a smirk before looking over toward Axel. "Hey Ax, should we go to dinner now?"

"Yeah. I'm starving! But can we come back here tomorrow to get started?" he says, sending hopeful eyes my way.

"Sure thing. We can plan where your room is going to be."

"You mean I can't have this one?" he asks, his forehead scrunched together.

"No, baby," April muses. "But you can pick the biggest one downstairs."

"Awesome," he shouts. He walks toward us, stopping right in front of me. "But Jamie, I've just got one last question."

"Yeah, buddy?" He tilts his head, stroking his chin like he's an old man stuck in a six-year-olds body. It's the most ridiculous image I've ever seen, but it's totally him.

Axel looks up at me and pulls his favorite puppy-dog-eyed look. "Dad boss, we need to talk about a raise."

I pull April and Axel into me before I burst out laughing.

"I don't know what's funny," he mumbles, which makes all of us adults chuckle.

It's fitting because, with Axel and April in my life, I think it's going to become a common occurrence.

And I can't fucking wait.

Work Violation
(Cook County #2)

Ronnie Nelson likes to be chased.
Jaxon Cook loves a challenge.

Ronnie wants a man who pulls out all the stops.
Jax doesn't stop until he gets what he wants.

Seems like a match made in heaven. Until an unexpected development makes their attraction away more complicated.

Now, committing a work violation has become a forgone conclusion and the chase just became a lot more complicated.

Lucky for Ronnie, Jax loves breaking the rules.

Lucky for Jax, Ronnie does too.

Pre-order at www.bjharveyauthor.com/books/work-violation/

Keep reading for Chapter 1 of Work Violation

Chapter 1

Jax

"Please join me and raise your glass to toast Jamie and April for their engagement, and for finally finishing their house. April, you're definitely a brave woman, taking him on, and remember, the most handsome Cook male is still single," I say, waggling my brows.

The crowd of our friends and family snicker. Jamie narrows his eyes at me, but his curved lips give him away. My big brother may seem like a moody son of a bitch but he's protective and loyal, and he's always one of the first people I call when I need something.

This house—*the* house—almost caused World War Three between us four brothers. There were even times April threatened Jamie with bodily harm if he didn't finish in time.

At least now that it's done, we can start our next project, our most ambitious yet: a two-story ex-bed-and-breakfast that has had years of neglect but holds a whole lot of promise. It's also pink... everywhere. Every room, every painted surface, even the garage trim—it's all magenta, fuchsia, and rose.

It's going to be a big job. Jamie and I decided before we closed on the property that it would only work if we were both working on it. Given I'm teaching a few college classes for the upcoming summer semester, it's ideal since I'll have guaranteed income. I won't have to be out there hustling for photography jobs, which means my time is free to help Jamie with the house, and I can live rent-free for three months. It's a win-win. Well, it will be.

After working their way through well-wishers, Jamie and April walk over to where I'm standing, April giving me a big hug when they reach me.

"Who knew you could give a good speech when you had to?" she says, tightening her arms around me. "Thank you, Jax."

I look over her shoulder to where Jamie is smiling at us, a look that soon morphs into a scowl when I run my hand down April's back toward her ass.

She giggles, Jamie growls, and I burst out laughing, tucking my soon-to-be sister-in-law under my arm, much to my brother's annoyance.

"You sure you want to marry this grump? I'm a lot more fun."

Jamie gently pries April out of my hold and back into his side. "Get your own woman."

I see April's lips twitch before she shoots me a wink. She tilts her head toward my brother and lifts a brow. "Your woman? Is that why you're marrying me? Me man, you woman?" she says, sounding like a caveman.

Jamie just smirks, hooking his hand around the back of her neck and crushing his mouth to hers, his tried and true way to shut her up when she starts sassing him.

April's best friend, Veronica—Ronnie—appears at Jamie's side, looking at the two lovebirds making out and rolling her eyes. "Do they ever stop sucking face?"

"Nope," I say, forcing myself to look away from her.

Over the past year, there have been many family events Ronnie has come along to. And every time, it's the same thing. I can't stop watching her. I just can't help admiring the view every time I see her. Ronnie has her own force field, and it's larger than life. She lights up a room the second she walks in.

We met in the front yard of our very first flipped house. I was covered in dirt and sweat, and April, Ronnie, and April's ex-mother-in-law had set up camp on April's front porch to watch us work. So naturally, since they wanted a show, I chose to give them one by peeling off my shirt.

I felt Ronnie's presence before I even saw her, and the moment I met her eyes, it was like I could see right into her soul.

Then I found out she was April's best friend and, well, that was the end of that. I was not going to do anything to cause problems for Jamie and his budding relationship with April. Not after he'd been through too much and finally had what he wanted within his grasp. So every time since that first meeting, I've forced myself to either act indifferent around her, or I've tried to ignore her completely. It's been a fool's errand though because she's not a woman any hot-blooded male could ignore.

But tonight, Ronnie is the personification of boho beautiful. I've tried to avoid her for most of the party, but with her standing here, smelling like summer nights and peaches, she's becoming harder and harder to resist.

"How have you been, Jax? It's been a while," she says, her warm voice reaching deep inside.

"Yeah, I'm good."

She elbows me gently, her gorgeous face now shining up at me, her smile huge. "It was a good speech. You might've just put yourself in the running to be Jamie's Best Man."

"I have my moments," I reply with a wink.

"I bet you do." The innuendo is definitely on point. "So what other talents are you hiding away?" Her sly smile and body leaning close to mine are doing crazy things to my brain, threatening my ability to think rationally. Needing to escape, I scan the yard to spot any other member of my family to use as an excuse to extricate myself from a conversation that could only end in disaster. Thankfully, April and Jamie rejoin the conversation.

"Ronnie, thank you so much for staying with Axel tonight. He lasted longer than I thought," April says. Axel is her six-year-old son, who I secretly want to kidnap. He's the coolest kid I've ever met because he's like a mini-me. He's now asleep upstairs in his brand new aviation-themed room. As the 'artist' in the family, Jamie asked me to design a bedroom that would make Axel the coolest kid in school. From the way the kid's eyes lit up and then filled with tears when he first saw the finished room, I'd say I met that goal. The added bonus is that I'm now his favorite uncle.

April turns to Ronnie. "How's school?"

"School?" I ask, my interest piqued.

Ronnie offers a small gift of a smile, a pink tinge blooms on her cheeks, which has me imagining other ways to make her blush. "Yeah, I had an 'I'm turning thirty-one and I don't like my life' crisis."

Jamie chuckles. "I had one of those at thirty-five. I think they can come at any age."

"I'm still so proud of you for doing that," April says, pulling Ronnie in for a hug.

"Let's see if it works out first. I may have given up a six-figure salary for nothing."

What the hell did she do for a job to earn *that* kind of money?

No. I don't need to know. My attraction to her miles of curves, long legs, dark blonde hair with the golden streaks threaded through, and her ruby-red lips that make me want to grab her and kiss her senseless, has never been rational. I've had to force myself to be outwardly indifferent, being standoffish to stop myself from entertaining thoughts of getting involved with her. With Jamie finally getting what he wants with April, I don't want to be the cause of any complications if things were to go wrong between Ronnie and myself.

"I need a drink," I announce sharply before spinning around and walking away towards the coolers storing all the alcohol.

I don't dare look back. That would be tempting fate, and I've got enough things to focus on without courting complications like Ronnie.

An hour later, I'm sitting in a corner by myself, a bottle of Jack and a bottle of cola my companions. The party is still going strong around me, the happy couple moving around the guests, my parents dancing in the middle of an imaginary dance floor, swaying side to side like they're the only ones in the room.

"You good?" my twin brother, Bryant, asks as he takes a seat beside me.

I slowly turn his way. "I'm good."

"Doesn't look like it."

I lift my half-full tumbler of whiskey to my mouth. "Jack and I are just fiiiine."

He chuckles. "Sounds like it. Give me some of that."

I slide the drinks his way and watch him pour the liquor.

"Cheers then," he says, knocking his glass to mine. "If you can't beat them, join them."

"Or if you can't touch them, get drunk and avoid them."

"What?" he asks with a startled laugh. "Who can't you touch and why the fuck not?"

My eyes drift across the yard to a laughing Ronnie who is standing with a group of Jamie's friends.

"Ahhh."

Dammit, the one time I wish he couldn't read me like a book.

"But why can't you touch if she wants you to?"

"What?" I ask, my movements a bit slower now as the Jack starts to take effect.

"Why can't that happen?"

"I don't need complications, and I definitely don't need to piss Jamie off by tapping and gapping his fiancée's best friend."

"Why would you tap and gap when you actually like her?"

"Slam and run?"

He grins. "How about jerk it and go back to work?" His lips twitch, and we both start chuckling. We're identical twins, Bryant being the older one, but there are differences between us. He has short, cropped, well-maintained hair; I lean towards the shaggy, creative, just-rolled-out-of-bed look. He's an assistant professor in biology; I'm a photographer who shoots sports and events, and takes the occasional road-trip for landscape shots.

"I think I'll just stay right here with my friends Jack and Coke, and *not* entertain thoughts of what might be with Ronnie. Why start something that could cause trouble if it didn't work out?"

"But what if it *did*?"

I look at him with a skeptical "don't go there" look.

"Alright. Just don't overdo it. You've got class on Monday, right?" the ever responsible Bryant says.

"Yep. Who would've thought we'd be teaching at the same college?" I snort. "In fact, who would've thought I'd be teaching at all?"

"You know you underestimate yourself, right? Your photos are amazing. You're super talented, and you wouldn't have been asked to teach those classes unless the powers that be thought you had something to offer."

I grunt in response, which just makes my brother laugh. "Since you're the resident sage today, what should I do about the other problem?"

"I think you should both get it out of your system and move on."

"What delusional universe are you living in that makes you think that would actually work?"

"A normal, adult one?"

"Ha fucking ha. Give me my Jack back and go be sociable."

"Like you are?"

"Yep. Call me Mr. Social Fucking Butterfly. I'm a ray of sunshine ready to brighten up the night."

Bry shakes his head and grins. "Okay. You've obviously caught the brood mood from Jamie. Have fun with Jack…" he says, pouring us both another drink before pushing his chair back and standing. "And if you actually want to get over this fixation you have with Miss Veronica, go make it happen, 'cause take it from me, the way she's been watching you all night, if you say go, she won't say no."

I frown up at him. "You're a poet, and you didn't even know it."

"Oh, I know it. How do you think I get laid so often?"

"Craigslist?" I ask with a smirk.

"Smartass," he mutters as he walks away.

My eyes drift back towards Ronnie, my gaze locking with hers and staying there. So many unspoken, filthy things are exchanged in just that look. She tilts her head toward the house, a sexy smirk playing on her lips. I quirk a brow, and her grin gets wider. Then I watch as she leans in and whispers something to April before skirting the edge of the group and scaling the stairs leading to the deck. Stopping at the back door, she glances over to me and licks her lips before disappearing in the house, and I know in that move that I'm done for.

Standing, I down my full glass in one go, now feeling decidedly blitzed as I cross the yard to follow her. It may not be a smart move, it may not be a good move, but following Ronnie into the house is the easiest decision I've made.

Maybe Bry is right. If we can just screw this lust out of our systems, we can just go on like everything's fine.

Once and done. Then happy families.

It should work, right?

Pre-order your copy of **Work Violation** at
www.bjharveyauthor.com/books/work-violation/

Want to know more about Abi and Cade?

Game Saver

From the USA Today bestselling author of the Bliss series comes a new spin off series featuring your favorite Bliss series characters who are yet to meet their match. Now it's Cade and Abi's turn.

How do you know when fake turns real?

Abi Cook lives her life by her own rules. She works hard, plays hard, and knows who she is and where she wants to be.

Following a repeat one-night stand with the dashing Dr. Cade Carsen, Cade asks Abi for a favor: be the fake girlfriend on his arm for the duration of his father's mayoral campaign.

Never one to turn down a challenge, she doesn't hesitate. I mean, who wouldn't when all that's involved is a little fake girlfriending with a side of hot sex, and with Doctor Hottie no less?

But like any Game, there are always twists and turns, unexpected players, villains, heroes and ultimately, winners and losers.

Game Saver is the story of what happens when two happily single people try for something less, but end up with something so much more.

Get **Game Saver** at www.bjharveyauthor.com/books/game-saver/

About the Author

BJ Harvey is the USA Today Bestselling Author of the Bliss Series. She also regards herself as a smut peddler, suspense conjurer and a funny romance thinker upper. An avid music fan, you will always find her singing some hit song badly but loving every minute of it. She's a wife, a mom to two beautiful girls, and hails from the best country in the world—New Zealand—but currently lives in Perth, Australia.

Facebook - www.facebook.com/bjharveyauthor
Instagram – www. instagram.com/bjharvs
Goodreads - www.goodreads.com/author/show/6886702.B_J_Harvey
Sign up for BJ's mailing list at www.eepurl.com/MfpyP

BJ HARVEY

Romantic Comedy
Bliss Series (Interconnected Standalones)

Temporary Bliss (Bliss #1)
True Bliss (Bliss #2)
Blissful Surrender (Bliss #3)
Permanent Bliss (Bliss #4)
Finding Bliss (Bliss #5)

The Game Series (Bliss Series Spin Off)

Game Player (Game #1)
Game Maker (Game #2)
Game Saver (Game #3)
Game Ender (Game #4)
Game Breaker (Game #5)
Game Planner (Game #6)

Holiday Romance
Stranded (Christmas novella with a Bliss Series connection)

Romance Suspense
Lost in Distraction (Lost #1)
Lost For You (Lost #2)
Lost Without You (Lost #3)

Other books by
BJ HARVEY

Contemporary Romance

One Shot (Chances #1)
Second Chance (Chances #2)
Third Strike (Chances #3)

Touch (Sovereign Part One)
Taste (Sovereign Part Two)
Feel (Sovereign Part Three)

CPSIA information can be obtained
at www.ICGtesting.com
Printed in the USA
LVHW030239160321
681607LV00008B/128